MAIA *and* HIPPOLYTA

by

JAMES A. PEREZ

BARROW COURT BOOKS

HUNTINGTON, NEW YORK

For my parents

CONTENTS

Blood and destruction shall be so in use
And dreadful objects so familiar
That mothers shall but smile when they behold
Their infants quarter'd with the hands of war;
All pity choked with custom of fell deeds:
And Caesar's spirit, ranging for revenge,
With Ate by his side come hot from hell,
Shall in these confines with a monarch's voice
Cry 'Havoc,' and let slip the dogs of war;
That this foul deed shall smell above the earth
With carrion men, groaning for burial.

Julius Caesar, Act 3, Scene 1
William Shakespeare (1564 – 1616)

MAIA *and* HIPPOLYTA

PROLOGUE

A MORE WORTHY OPPONENT

THE DEMI-GOD KICKED the fallen warrior as her final breath rattled in her throat.

"Pathetic," he spat. "Is there no creature more worthy?"

Beyond the forest at the edge of the battlefield, a horse whinnied and took to a gallop.

The demi-god called, "I know there are more of you out there! Your queen will be abashed to learn you hid rather than fight!"

A young man in armor sprayed with blood ran towards the demi-god. He laid his sword and shield on the ground and kneeled before speaking.

"My lord, our scouts say the queen is on the move. We can catch her if we act quickly!"

The demi-god reached out and grabbed the young man by the throat, lifting him off his feet.

"You say, 'our' scouts? 'We' can catch her? There is no 'we,' boy," the demi-god growled before he hurled the young man against the trunk of a nearby tree.

CRACK!

The young man crumbled to the ground, his body but a sack of broken glass.

"Come," the demi-god called to his remaining men. "Perhaps the queen will present more of a challenge."

"And... and if she does not, my lord?" asked one of the men, his head bowed.

"Then I continue to search until I find an opponent worth the interest of the son of Zeus."

CHAPTER 1

ANOTHER LETTER

MAIA PETERSON SLAMMED her locker closed. Groaning, she picked up an envelope that had fallen to the floor. It was unopened and had been so since delivered to Maia during homeroom. She held it at arm's length as if the envelope might bite.

"Hey, Maia!"

Through the crowd of students, Maia saw her best friend, Jackie, approaching. Her ever-present smile quickly turned to a frown when she saw the unopened envelope in Maia's hand.

"You haven't read it?"

"No."

"What are you waiting for? You're the first one to get a letter. I thought you'd be busting to open it."

"Yeah, well, what if I wasn't accepted?"

"Of course you were accepted. You were made for the youth ambassadorship program. And it's in Greece! How much more perfect can it get?"

"Jackie—"

"No. I can't listen to any more excuses," said Jackie, folding her arms.

Few people knew Maia as well as Jackie. They'd been friends since kindergarten and endured together the many trials of a public school education. If anyone could get Maia to open the envelope, it'd be Jackie.

"Hey, MVP!" called a boy in a varsity football jacket as he passed Maia.

"See! You're like one of the most popular girls in school since the lacrosse team won the all-county championship. You definitely got in."

"I don't think they care about popularity or athletic skills when they choose youth ambassadors," Maia countered.

"You'll never know unless you—"

"Fine," Maia said, allowing her body to fall against her locker. "I'll open it."

Jackie squealed. Maia rolled her eyes at her friend and drew a deep breath. She turned the envelope over and slid her finger under the corner of the flap. She looked up at Jackie again before going any further.

"What if—"

"Oh, give me that," Jackie said as she grabbed the letter away from Maia. Before Maia could stop her, Jackie tore the envelope open and pulled out a letter.

"Okay, let's see... *blah, blah, blah...* "

"Jackie, give it back!"

"Oh, alright. I'm sure you'll be disappointed to know that you got in," Jackie said.

"What?"

Jackie burst out laughing. "You got in! You're going to be a youth ambassador to Greece this summer!"

Jackie handed Maia the letter. Her hands shook as she read it, wrinkling the paper.

"Wow."

"That's all you have to say? Maia, you're finally going back to Greece! Isn't that what you've wanted?"

Good question, Maia thought. It'd been three years since Maia made her first journey to the country in which she'd been born. Of course, Maia only discovered that she hadn't been born in her small seaside village of Sea Cliff, Long Island a few weeks before she'd made the trip. But that was hardly the biggest revelation that summer.

Through a simultaneously thrilling and terrifying series of events, Maia had learned that the mythological gods of Olympus were, in fact, real. The gods survived over the centuries by creating a hidden world called Olympia, a perfect replica of ancient Greece where they continued to reign – where sightings of winged horses and mermaids were quite common. Maia had been made to travel to Olympia, and once there she made the painful discovery that her long-lost father, a native of Olympia, had sacrificed himself to protect the hidden world shortly after her birth.

Maia glanced down at the heavy bracelet of gold on her wrist. It was a gift from Zeus, king of the gods of Olympus, and it was meant to protect her from being taken back to Olympia against her will. Maia ran her fingers over the bracelet. She circled a symbol of wings with her index finger.

"So, what do you think your mom will say?"

It was another good question, one to which Maia didn't have a quick answer. Maia's mother was often unpredictable when it came to these types of situations.

"Do you mean before or after she flogs me for not telling her I applied to the program?"

"How could she be mad? She knows you've wanted to go back to Greece, and now you can. Does the letter say anything about the scholarship you applied for?" asked Jackie.

Maia had entirely forgotten about how she was going to pay for the trip. Her eyes moved up and down the wrinkled sheet of paper until she found what she was looking for in the last paragraph.

"They're going to pay for my airfare," Maia said, showing Jackie the letter.

"That's great! You'll just need spending money."

"Yeah, I guess."

"Maia, I don't understand you!" Jackie blurted. "You're acting as if you don't want to go."

"Of course I want to go. It's just that I should've said something to my mother sooner."

"It'll be fine. Come on, we're going to be late for work."

Since September, Maia and Jackie worked a few days after school at the Sea Cliff Village Library. While it'd originally been Jackie's idea to apply for jobs, it was Maia who truly treasured the experience, especially now that lacrosse season was over and the school year was coming to an end. Despite the thrill of leading her team to a county championship, Maia was glad to have more time on her hands to earn money. The library was also a place of special importance. It always brought Maia fond memories of when her mother would take her there as a young girl.

"Do you need anything from your locker?" Maia asked Jackie, noticing that she was missing her backpack.

"Oh, yeah. I'll be right back," said Jackie, brushing past a harried teacher balancing a stack of books.

"I'll meet you by the office," Maia called.

Maia maneuvered her way through the packed hallway. A few students yelled, "MVP!" – short for both "Most Valuable Player" and Maia Victoria Peterson. Squeezing around a boy pushing a cello case, Maia stopped in front of a glass display cabinet holding the girls' lacrosse championship trophy.

"Admiring your handiwork?"

Maia looked up at the reflection of her school counselor, Mr. Foster. She hadn't realized he was standing behind her.

"Hey, Mr. Foster," Maia said, turning to face him.

"So, I gave a letter to your homeroom teacher to give to you this morning. I was expecting to see you at some point soon afterwards."

"I just opened it."

"And?" Mr. Foster asked.

"I got in."

"Outstanding! What about the scholarship?"

"Airfare is covered," Maia answered.

"Maia, that's great! I bet you can't wait to tell your mother."

Maia looked at the maroon and brown tile floor.

"Yeah, I'm sure she's going to be thrilled," she said.

"Maia, you need to give your mother more credit than that. I know she's busy working a lot, but—"

"Hey, Foster!" interrupted Jackie. "Did Maia tell you the good news?"

"Yes, Miss Tam, we were just talking about it. I'm sorry, but I have to run to track practice. Maia, come see me tomorrow during study hall," said Mr. Foster. "We can talk more about the program."

"Okay," Maia responded, forcing a smile.

"Foster is the best," Jackie gushed as the school counselor was swallowed by the crowd.

"Yeah. Maybe he'll know how to convince my mom to let me go."

"She's going to be fine," Jackie said. "Everything is going to work out."

Jackie talked nonstop as they made the rather long walk from Sea Cliff High School to the library, but Maia was glad for the distraction. It helped to push away the crushing question occupying her thoughts. How *would* her mother react? When Maia returned from Greece three years ago, her relationship with her mother grew stronger and closer. Though she never told her mother about her adventures in Olympia, her experiences there seemed to have yielded a profound effect on her mother as well.

A year later, Maia's grandfather became very ill, and, after six months of visits back and forth to the hospital, he passed away quietly in his sleep. Maia's mother, a pediatric nurse, was forced to take on extra shifts at work to pay for Grandpa's medical bills. Soon, their relationship was back to where it'd once been, with Maia craving her mother's attention but trying her best to hide her disappointment when it wasn't available.

"Maia, are you listening to me?" Jackie asked.

"Sorry. I was just thinking. What did you say?"

"Are you going to let your family in Greece know?"

"Don't you think I should find out if I'm actually going first?"

Jackie stuck her tongue out. "I bet your cousin Helena will be happy to see you, and your grandmother and uncles too. What was the name of your favorite uncle?"

"Dorian."

"Right. You must be psyched to see them all again."

"Jackie—"

"No! I don't want to hear any more negativity," Jackie interrupted. "And you better be happy for me when I get my letter. God, I hope I got in!"

Maia recognized a familiar far-off look in Jackie's eyes. She was more excited than Maia about the trip. Like many times before, Maia contemplated whether to tell Jackie the truth about her father. Maia told no one, and it was a strain that caused her lots of sleepless nights.

"I'm sure you got in," said Maia.

"Do you really think so? That would be so amazing!"

And again, Jackie was off. She talked the rest of the way to the library and all through their shift. The librarian shushed her twice. As they finished stacking a pile of picture books, Maia slammed one down on a shelf.

"Jackie! What's gotten into you? You haven't stopped talking for hours. It's like you're possessed or on something."

"I'm just excited, that's all," Jackie said. "I mean, shouldn't at least one of us be?"

Maia sucked in air through her teeth. "Yeah, you're right. After we get out of here, do you want to come to my house for a while?"

"Yeah, sure," Jackie said, tapping Maia on the head with a book of nursery rhymes.

"Jackie," said the librarian, "you have a phone call."

Jackie looked at Maia with one raised eyebrow before marching over to the reference desk. Maia focused on the pile of picture books. She picked up one with winged horses on the cover. Her thoughts traveled back to Olympia and a winged horse named Pierinos that helped save her from Aeton, a particularly cruel man with a beard as dark as his heart. Maia was flipping through the book when Jackie trotted over.

"I have to go," Jackie said. "Something came up, and my parents need me to watch my brother."

"It's okay," Maia said. "We can hang out tomorrow."

"Are you sure?"

"Yeah, don't worry about it."

After she gathered her belongings, Jackie waved to Maia as she exited the library. Maia admitted to a mix of disappointment and relief. She'd been very close to telling Jackie about Olympia, but it was better she didn't – at least not yet. Maia still had to talk to her mother, and, until she knew the outcome of that conversation, there was a good possibility she wouldn't be returning to Greece at all.

CHAPTER 2

NEVER BEEN THE SAME

MAIA SAT ON HER front porch, strumming her guitar. She played the same chords over and over again, never quite satisfied with the sound. Maia swept the strings and smacked the body of the guitar, making a loud thud.

"That's lovely," said her neighbor Mrs. Tuttle, as she planted a variety of red and yellow flowers in front of her house.

"Oh, thanks."

Maia plucked the strings of her guitar, letting the last note carry before mustering the courage to ask Mrs. Tuttle if she wanted to hear a song she'd written.

"Of course, dear. I would love to."

Maia closed her eyes and began to play the song she'd been working on for the past few months. Cautious at first, but growing in confidence, Maia threw herself into the song, as she was prone to do. There were words she'd written to go with the music, but Maia hummed along instead. There was no sense in arousing Mrs. Tuttle's curiosity about the meaning of the lyrics. Maia reached the chorus, the words for which came to her one sleepless night:

> *Struck down*
> *I watched him fall, I watched him fall*
> *Struck down*
> *No mercy from the waves*

Struck down
I watched him fall, I watched him fall
Struck down
I've never been the same

The sensations bound to watching Icarus, the boy who first took her to Olympia, fall to the sea were as raw as they were three years ago. Every so often, a breeze from the harbor would catch Maia as she passed Memorial Park on her way home, the smell of brine bringing her back to the horror of his loss and the fear that she too would be consumed by the waves.

Maia finished the song. For a moment, she allowed herself to really think about Icarus. He drove her crazy at first, but by the end of her adventure in Olympia her feelings had changed. And then he fell.

"That was wonderful, Maia!" Mrs. Tuttle gushed. "What do you call it?"

"I haven't come up with a title yet."

"Well, I really enjoyed it. You should—"

RING!

"Oh, excuse me, Maia. That could be my daughter calling." Mrs. Tuttle brushed the dirt from her clothes and hurried into her house.

Maia set her guitar down into its case. Playing music could put her at ease, but on this occasion she still felt a pang of worry. It seemed so logical – if not cowardly – at the time not to tell her mother and to wait for the outcome of her application to the international youth ambassadorship program, but now Maia could only foretell an argument. And who could blame her mother for being angry?

The sight of her mother's car turning onto their block and pulling into the driveway interrupted Maia's imaginary familial clash. Her mother stepped out of the car. She didn't seem to notice Maia at first, but when mother and daughter locked eyes it was clear from the expression on Mrs. Peterson's face that it was going to be anything but a quiet evening at the dinner table.

"How was school today, sweetie? Did anything exciting happen? Any interesting letters?"

"Mom, I—"

"Maia, why didn't you tell me?" Mrs. Peterson asked, shaking her head.

"Tell you what?"

"Your counselor called me, and he... Maia, what's the look for?"

"I wish Mr. Foster hadn't done that," Maia said.

"Why? Maia, you've been talking about going back to Greece for the last three years. I'm just... I'm just so proud of you."

Maia shifted her feet. Her left ankle still ached from a hit she took at the end of the last game of the county championship.

"You're not mad? You want me to go?"

"Of course I do. If I could've sent you back to Greece, I would've done it already. This is an amazing... why are you laughing?"

"Oh, come on. Don't you think this is even a little bit funny? Last time, I had to convince *you* to let me go."

"A lot has changed since that summer," Maia's mother said.

Maia felt another shot of pain – not in her ankle, but in her side, just like any time she allowed her mind to linger on the summer after seventh grade. It's 'psychosomatic,' Maia reminded herself, copping a term she learned in her psychology elective class.

"Maia?"

"What? Oh, sorry."

"If you're having any doubts—"

"No, I do want to go."

Another twinge, sharper and longer.

"Tomorrow, I'll drop you off at school, and then I'll go see Mr. Foster about whatever papers you obviously forged my signature on."

"Actually, Jackie signed your name," Maia said, shrugging her shoulders.

"Really? And is she going to Greece too?" Maia's mother asked.

"She hasn't heard back yet."

"Do her parents know? Or did you sign her application?"

"They know. There was a meeting for parents about it at school," said Maia.

"Oh, great. I must look like 'Mother of the Year' for skipping that. Did you at least come up with a good excuse?"

"I think I said you were bowling."

"That's the best you could come up with?"

Maia giggled. "Thanks for not being angry, Mom."

"For what? Making people think I bowl?"

"Yes, I mean, no. I mean, thanks for everything. I thought you wouldn't let me go."

"Maia, as much as I want to keep you safe and protected under my wings, I know that I have to let you fly away sometimes."

Maia hugged her mother, grateful for her understanding though wishing she'd chosen a different analogy than one involving wings. As she held onto her mother, Maia's side ached worse than ever before, but somehow (at least for the moment) it didn't matter. She was going back to Greece!

CHAPTER 3

AN UNSAVORY VISITOR

WALKING HOME FROM SCHOOL had never seemed to take so long as the day Jackie received her acceptance letter to the youth ambassadorship program.

"Oh, my god, oh, my god, oh, my god! This is going to be amazing! What do you think the other ambassadors will be like? Oh, my god! We're actually going to Greece!"

"Jackie! You need to calm down. If you're going to act this way for the next four weeks, I'm not going on the trip," Maia said.

"Oh, whatever," Jackie replied. "Maybe if you keeping acting that way, I won't go."

"I seriously doubt that."

"Ha! I know, but come on already. Your mom was totally cool with the whole thing. There's no reason for you to not be as excited as I am."

"Yeah, I know but—"

"Is it because of that boy?"

"Jackie, I've told you a million times – there was no boy."

"And I've told you a million times – you talk in your sleep. The first time you slept at my house after you got back from Greece, you kept talking about a boy."

"If I did, it was probably about one of my cousins. I've got tons," Maia said.

"Did one of them die?"

"Jackie!"

"What?"

"There are some things about my trip I'm still not ready to talk about. And now that I'm going back, I'm not sure what to feel. If you really are my best friend and you care about me, then you'll just have to cut me some slack. I'm excited. I honestly am, but I'm nervous too. It's complicated."

"Sorry. I was being a jerk," Jackie said.

"No, you weren't. I've been weird about this whole thing. It's not your fault."

"Have you ever tried telling someone about whatever happened over there?"

"Once. But I didn't even know where to start. Anyway, it doesn't matter. I can deal with it," Maia said as they stopped in front of Jackie's house. "Do you want to get together to study for the English final later? I don't think I can tackle another monologue from *Julius Caesar* on my own."

"Yeah, maybe. I just have to check with my folks. Sam's been giving them a hard time lately. With the trip coming up, I want to help out as much as I can."

"What about Zack? How come he's never around?"

Jackie had two brothers. Zack was graduating from high school in a few days. Sam was in middle school. He was the first child diagnosed with autism that Maia had ever known. When he was younger, he loved being around Maia and Jackie, and he used to follow them incessantly. But now, Maia hardly ever saw either of Jackie's brothers.

"Zack's too busy with his girlfriend. They have just a couple more months together... *blah, blah, blah*," Jackie said, pretending to gag. "I'll call you later."

"Okay, tell Sam I said hi."

"I will. Thanks."

Jackie entered her house. There was no one else on the block besides Maia.

"The boy's name was Icarus," Maia said, "and he died to save me."

Feeling somewhat less burdened after her admission, Maia started off for home. Jackie was a good friend, but Maia doubted that anyone could understand (or believe her) if she talked about Olympia. There were times that Maia thought she imagined the whole experience or at least wished that she did. Icarus wasn't the only one to die protecting Maia. There was also the guard, Ophelos. He took an arrow to the chest. Before she escaped from Olympia, Maia watched two people fall, but it wasn't until months later that she allowed herself to think about their deaths. Not so often, Maia's mother would come home from the hospital and talk about a patient that died. Mrs. Peterson was devastated every time it happened. This made Maia feel even worse that such a long stretch of time passed before she shed a tear for Icarus or Ophelos. She knew nothing about Ophelos. Did he have a family? Icarus had a father named Daedalus. But he didn't even seem to care when Maia told him that Icarus had fallen into the sea. "Actions have a way of repeating themselves in Olympia," Zeus said, confusing the matter further. Could Icarus have survived?

There was a third person for whose death Maia felt responsible, though he died long before Maia had been taken to Olympia. Her father left her and her mother before Maia could form a memory of him. But there were many others who remembered him in Olympia and for good reason. He'd sacrificed himself to keep Maia and her world safe. Learning of his demise had left Maia with more questions than answers and with few people available to offer any assistance. Returning to Greece – and to Olympia as well, perhaps – was a chance to seek out more information about her father.

"*Ow!*" Maia yelped. Her bracelet was burning her skin. She pulled it off and threw it to the ground where it made a brown circle in the grass. Despite it being a gift from a god, nothing strange like that had ever happened before. Maia took a bottle of water out of her backpack and poured it over the bracelet. Once the steam dissipated, Maia tapped the bracelet with her finger. It was still warm, but no longer burning hot. After waiting a minute, Maia picked up the bracelet and quickly dropped it again – not out of pain but from surprise. There was a new symbol on the bracelet, next to that of the pair of wings that had been there from the beginning. It was a sword.

"What the hell?" Maia muttered.

A car blasting music passed Maia before screeching to a halt. "Hey, Maia! What are you looking at?" It was Jackie's brother Zack.

"Hi, Zack. I just dropped... my keys," Maia said as she scooped up the bracelet and put it in her pocket.

"Do you need a ride?"

"No, my house is right... " But Maia was nowhere near her house. She was by the harbor, blocks away from where she remembered being when her bracelet began to burn her.

"Are you okay?" Zack asked.

"Yeah. Um, you know, I will take a ride."

Thankfully, Zack began blasting music as soon as Maia got in his car, allowing her to avoid conversation. Maia rubbed her wrist. The skin was red from the bracelet, but it was her side that truly hurt. Zack pulled in front of Maia's house and with a nod sped off once Maia stepped onto the sidewalk.

On her porch, Maia fumbled for her keys, nearly dropping them from how much her hands were shaking. She opened and slammed the door closed as quickly as she could. Leaning against a small table, Maia reached into her pocket and took out the bracelet. The sword was still there. She slipped the bracelet onto her wrist. It was then that she noticed an unsavory smell coming from the living room.

"Mom, are you home?"

No one answered. Maia clutched her keys between her fingers and moved down the hall. The living room was empty. Maia turned to go upstairs and let out a shriek as she smashed into a man wearing robes splattered with blood.

"Aftós sas periménei."

Maia stepped back and swung her fist holding the keys, but the man blocked her and pushed her to the floor. He grabbed Maia's bracelet and pressed it hard enough to dig into her skin.

"You must prepare yourself, child. He is waiting for you. The son of Zeus will not idle long," Maia understood the man to say before he held up his fist and squeezed it.

There was a bright flash of light. Maia squinted and rubbed her eyes. The man was gone, but his words hung in the air like a butcher's knives. Someone in Olympia was expecting her. Maia jumped to her feet and bounded up the stairs to her room. Sitting on her bed, Maia pressed her thumb on the symbol of the sword on her bracelet. Not without a fight, Maia swore. If the son of Zeus wanted to take her down, she wasn't going to fall so easily.

CHAPTER 4

A TROUBLING CONVERSATION

MAIA HAD GIVEN THOUGHT to calling her Uncle Dorian in Greece several times over the years, but she always managed to talk herself out of it. What was there to say? Maia had left things with her family in Greece on the best terms possible – at least the best that could be expected from a teenager whose family had been keeping a score of secrets from her that nearly resulted in her death. There'd been a few letters exchanged with her grandmother and her cousin Helena, but that was it. Uncle Dorian had kept his distance, and Maia appreciated that to a large extent.

Maia cradled the telephone in her hand. She'd already dialed and hung up twice when the telephone surprised her by ringing.

"Hello? No, you have the wrong number. Yes, I'm sure. This isn't a pizzeria."

Maia allowed herself to laugh if ever so briefly. Without further wavering, Maia dialed Uncle Dorian's telephone number. After a series of clicks, the telephone began to ring. The oddness of the sound was distracting, and Maia was frankly surprised when someone picked up on the other end of the line.

"Parakalo."

"Hi, Uncle Dorian. It's, um, it's Maia."

There were a few seconds of silence. Maia clenched her teeth.

"Hello, Maia. This is most unexpected. How are you?"

Fine. Terrified. Angry. Any one of those adjectives would do.

"I've been better. Uncle Dorian, is anything going on in... you know, the other place?"

Again, silence.

"Why do you ask?"

"Because I had a visitor the other day. And unless robes splattered with blood are becoming popular summer wear in Sea Cliff, I think he may have traveled some distance."

"I see you have not lost your wit."

"Uncle Dorian, this wasn't an easy phone call to make. I'm asking for your help, and I think I'm entitled to it. Before I come back to Greece, I need—"

"You are coming to Greece?"

"Yes. In a few weeks."

"Do you think that is wise?"

"I wasn't sure about it even before... one of *your* people showed up in my living room. Now I definitely don't think it's a good idea, but I'm still coming. What's going on 'over there' that I should know about?"

"Maia, before I answer that, I must ask you a question. Have you removed the bracelet given to you by Lord Zeus?" asked Uncle Dorian.

"I did just a short while before this all happened. I had to because it was burning me. And then a new symbol appeared – a sword," said Maia.

"Pay the symbol no mind. Are you wearing the bracelet now?"

"Yes."

"Do not take it off again. Maia, you should not come to Greece. There is always unrest on the other side, but there must be more afoot than I realized for this to have befallen you."

"I'm not afraid. I just want to know what to expect."

"If you keep the bracelet on, you should expect nothing more. I will call you once I have more information," said Uncle Dorian.

"I'm leaving in three weeks," Maia said. "If I don't hear back from you, I'm getting on the plane."

"Maia, if I am not soon in contact with you, then you must certainly not come. I must go. Goodbye."

Maia held the telephone to her ear for several seconds after Uncle Dorian hung up. When she finally placed it back in the cradle, she saw how sweaty her palm had become during the call. Uncle Dorian could scarcely hide his alarm. "Unrest," he'd said. Likely an understatement given that three years ago, when Maia was brought to Olympia the second time, a pair of catty crows – after they'd made fun of her clothes – told her about a war brewing between the gods.

Maia peered at the doorway between her kitchen and dining room. She sniffed the air for any trace of the smell the man in robes had left behind. Maia's mother hadn't mentioned anything out of the ordinary when she came home that day, leading Maia to think she may have imagined the smell and that it was something she alone would have sensed. It was impossible to fathom all of the strange rules and workings surrounding Olympia and its denizens. Even her bracelet gave her pause. All of this time, Maia trusted in the bracelet's power to keep her safe from recognition – in her own world and in Olympia. But would it allow her to travel between the two? Like the man in her living room, most of those who made the trek relied on a tool that emitted a bright flash of light. Maia never saw the tool up close, but she'd felt its blinding effect countless times.

Maia looked at the clock. Her mother wouldn't be home for at least another hour. She skipped out of the door in her kitchen leading to the backyard. Maia opened a small shed and picked up her lacrosse stick and a ball. Standing in the center of the back-yard, Maia threw the ball against a rebounder net guarding the back fence. Catching the ball after it rebounded, Maia threw it again, keeping this back and forth going for a lengthy stretch of time without a break – and without missing a single rebound.

"Pretty impressive."

Maia spun and threw the ball in the direction of the voice. Jackie's brother Zack ducked and just barely avoided being pegged in the head.

"Whoa! Take it easy, MVP. I just came by to give you this. I think you left it in my car the other day," Zack said, holding out a small leather-bound book with decorative gold tooling.

Maia leaned her lacrosse stick next to a wooden bench.

"That's not mine."

"Are you sure? I asked Jackie, and she said it could be yours."

"It's not, but I'll bring it to the library tomorrow," Maia said as she turned the book over. "Where *is* Jackie? She didn't come to work today."

"Yeah, it's kind of crazy at our house right now. Our parents don't know what to do with Sam. Jackie is helping out. I am too, but she and Sam have a special relationship. She can get him to do things that the rest of us can't."

"Well, when you talk to her, tell her to call me," Maia said.

After Zack left, Maia sat down on the bench and flipped through the book. Adding to the mystery, she realized that the contents were written in Greek. It definitely wasn't a library book. As she flipped through it a second time, a folded-up piece of paper fell out of the book and onto the floor. Maia unfolded the paper. It was covered with a drawing of a girl holding a sword. Maia compared the drawing to the symbol on her bracelet. They were very similar, almost to the point of matching. And the girl, though crudely drawn, resembled Maia as well.

Maia leaned over and picked up her lacrosse stick. Standing, Maia held the stick upside down, grasping it just above the head. She glanced at the drawing. Doing her best to match the stance of the girl, Maia swung the stick. Holding her arms out straight, Maia swung the stick again and again. Staring at some imaginary opponent, Maia jabbed the stick forward and held it for several seconds before letting it drop to the ground. Not ready to wield a sword against the son of Zeus, Maia thought, but a decent beginning.

CHAPTER 5

TO TELL THE TRUTH

THE CROWD AT John F. Kennedy International Airport was a medley of accents and aromas, making it difficult for Maia to give her mother her full attention as she went through a lengthy list of last minute rules and reminders.

"Passport?"

"Check."

"Boarding pass?"

"Check."

"Overbearing mother?"

"Ha ha."

"You're not enjoying this at all, are you?" Maia mother's asked.

"As long as you are, Mom, that's all that matters," Maia said.

"This is how we say goodbye? A little less sarcasm would go a long way," Mrs. Peterson responded.

"Sorry. I'm more nervous than I thought I'd be."

"You're going to be a great ambassador, Maia. And you'll have fun too," Maia's mother offered. "Do you have your uncle's phone number?"

"Yeah, I wrote it on an index card. I'm using it to hold my place," Maia said, pulling a book from her backpack.

"Is that for the plane? I doubt Jackie is going to give you much peace and quiet."

"Tell me about it," Maia said as Jackie pranced around the airport newsstand. "I've never seen her this excited. No, I take that back. There was that time she found a 'buffalo nickel' on the sidewalk."

"Maia, keep spewing all that acid, and you'll burn a hole through your tongue. What are you reading?"

"It's called *The True Story of Greek Mythology*. I thought it might be practical."

"If you run into a god, I suppose," Maia's mother quipped.

"Now who's doing the mocking?"

"I'm not. Well, maybe a little. Never mind that. Call your uncle. I tried his number again this morning before you woke up, and I still couldn't get him."

Maia internally shared in her mother's displeasure. Uncle Dorian hadn't called Maia back. But she wasn't letting that stop her from going to Greece even if she assumed something grave had happened to him. Maia wore her bracelet, and she had no reason to doubt the promise that came with it from Zeus – although his son didn't seem to have her best interests at heart.

Maia looked up at the screen listing departures. Saying good-bye to her mother was harder than she'd anticipated, but she and Jackie still needed to get through security, and the line was characteristically long.

"I guess we should go," Maia said.

"I'm going to miss you, sweetie," Maia's mother said as she wrapped her arms around her and squeezed tight enough for Maia to let out a heavy lungful.

"Me too, Mom. Thanks for letting me go. I love you."

Before Mrs. Peterson could respond to Maia's happily welcomed expression of feeling, Jackie came running over with a plastic bag filled with magazines and an exceptionally large bar of chocolate.

"Is it time? I'm sorry. I didn't know how many magazines I should buy," Jackie squeaked.

"I think you should be covered. You can watch a movie too," Maia's mother said. "Have a safe trip. Call me when you can, Maia."

After another round of hugs, Maia and Jackie joined the long queue leading to the security checkpoint. Maia took a moment to appreciate how much trust her mother had in her, allowing her and Jackie to navigate the airport essentially unsupervised. Youth ambassadors were coming from all over the United States and other countries as well, so it wasn't possible for them all to be chaperoned. An uncomfortable wave of guilt washed over Maia knowing that her mother would be horrified if she knew where her trust in her daughter was getting her. Once in Greece, Maia had every intention of returning to Olympia.

* * *

JACKIE FELL ASLEEP twenty minutes into the flight from New York City to Athens, leaving Maia the opportunity to sample her magazines and chocolate bar. After familiarizing herself with the latest Hollywood breakups and potential blockbuster summer movies, Maia flipped through her book. The author of *The True Story of Greek Mythology* started off with a broad claim that everything from the Trojan horse to the authorship of *The Odyssey* by Homer was likely fiction. Maia read on for a while until she came to a long section on Daedalus. Again the author maintained that the renowned inventor and his son, Icarus, were probably made up, and Daedalus's numerous achievements were likely attributed to him for the sake of consistency once the legends of Greece began to be recorded. An interesting theory, Maia thought. However, having met the man and wanted to throttle him, she could attest that not only was Daedalus a gifted artificer, but he was also an arrogant and cold-hearted jackass.

By the time the pilot announced that they'd soon begin to make their descent into Athens International Airport, Maia had read most of the book and gotten very little sleep. Jackie, on the other hand, was completely well rested and buzzing with excitement. Maia leaned her head against the wall of the airplane and watched the plumes of clouds thin out to the occasional white wisp as land became more readily visible. Greece – the place of her birth and greatest heartache – was within sight.

"Jackie, do you see that? Isn't it beau—"

"Maia! Did you eat my chocolate bar?"

"Well, before you judge me, I don't think it was fair of you to fall asleep and not consider the possibility that I'd take a piece or two."

"You ate the whole thing!"

"I'll buy you another one when we land," Maia offered. "Look out the window."

"Can you see any ruins?"

"Um, maybe a couple," Maia kidded.

"What's the place in Athens with all the temples?"

"It's called the Acropolis. That's where the Parthenon is."

"Where the gods once walked."

"What did you say?" asked Maia.

"I said, 'where the gods once walked.' Isn't that what you told me about the Acropolis when you came back from Greece three years ago?" Jackie asked.

"Yeah, I guess I did," Maia said, turning to the window.

The pilot came on the cabin speaker and announced their descent along with the stock reminders about seatbelts and tray tables. Maia put her book in her backpack and gathered up any shreds of chocolate bar wrapper. Moments later, the wheels of the airplane touched the tarmac with a jolt that matched the intense pounding of Maia's heart. It was almost beating loud enough to drown out the noise of the passengers as they prepared to depart the airplane.

"Maia, are you ready to go?"

Leave it to Jackie to save her most challenging question for their last seconds on the airplane. With an expression that couldn't convey the full range of emotions she was experiencing, Maia stated, "Yes, I'm ready."

CHAPTER 6

THE OTHER OLYMPIA

THE BUS DOOR OPENED with a hiss. Maia wrinkled her nose as a scent not dissimilar from raw onions wafted in her direction.

"Is this the bus for the youth ambassadors?" she asked, secretly hoping it wasn't.

"Nai, nai," answered the bus driver. "This is bus for youth ambassadors."

"Maia, what's that smell?"

"Shhh, Jackie. I don't think the bus is air conditioned."

The driver lugged himself out of his seat, his feet hammering the steps of the bus. The driver pulled down his shirt covering his ample belly, and with a tip of his hat said, "I take suitcases. You go sit."

"Thank you," Maia said, flinging her backpack over her shoulder.

"Are we supposed to tip him?" Jackie asked as she followed Maia up the steps.

The smell Maia had detected before was even stronger on board. She tugged at the collar of her shirt, tempted to pull it over her nose.

"The air conditioner isn't working," said a boy wearing an Oakland A's baseball cap in the third row of seats. "And you have a lousy poker face."

Embarrassed by her obviousness, Maia managed a little smirk and shuffled past the boy with an easily audible, "You have lousy taste in ball clubs."

"He's cute," Jackie gushed as she sat next to Maia in the second to last row. "I don't think he liked what you said."

"I guess I have to work on my people skills if I'm going to be an ambassador. What is with this window? It's either stuck or—"

"The windows do not open."

The voice came from the seats in front of them. Maia hadn't noticed anyone sitting there as she passed. A boy sat up and turned to face her, pushing his shaggy blonde hair out of his eyes. Maia detected mischief radiating from his face.

"I am Roc," said the boy, "from Barcelona. That is in Spain."

"Yes, I know that. You have a good soccer team."

"Ah, you like fútbol?"

"Yes, but she's a fantastic lacrosse player," Jackie chirped.

"Lacrosse? What is that? You chase each other with a long stick," Roc said with a scowl. "No, the true sport is fútbol."

Maia felt her hands searching for a lacrosse stick to swing. "Have you ever played lacrosse?"

"Eh? No, I must not waste time with such things. If you like, I will show you how to play my sport," said Roc, nodding his head.

"Well, as kind an offer as that is, I think you should probably turn around. Looks like we're leaving."

Roc cocked his head and narrowed his eyes like a cat first noticing a mouse poking around the corner of a room. "You are from America."

"Yes. And you're from Spain, so I'm guessing your flight wasn't quite as long as ours. I'm really tired. Sorry, Block, but can we pick this up another time?"

"Of course," answered Roc. Turning around, he added, "I look forward to it. And my name is Roc."

Jackie elbowed Maia once Roc's blonde mane was completely out of sight. "Wow, he's cute too. Did you think there were going to be so many good-looking guys in the program?"

Before Maia could answer, the bus hit a bump, and she knocked her head on the seatback in front of her.

"Well, that happened," Maia said, squinting.

"Please, some of us try to sleep," Roc called.

"*Pffft!*" snickered Jackie.

"Et tu, Jackie?"

"Sorry, but I thought he was funny," Jackie said with a shrug.

"Gracias," called Roc again.

Maia rubbed her head as she counted off ways of using a soccer ball to inflict bodily harm. Sinking back, Maia's eyes closed of their own will. She would practice her diplomatic skills when she didn't feel so ragged.

* * *

AFTER A FEW MORE BUMPS in the road, Maia accepted that she wasn't destined to remain asleep, and she slowly blinked her way back to consciousness.

"Jackie, how long have I been asleep?"

No answer. The seat next to Maia's was empty, but Jackie's voice could be heard from the row in front of her. That didn't take long, Maia thought. Her cousin Helena would be proud, if not jealous, of Jackie's speed in chatting up a boy.

Maia's backpack rattled in the storage compartment above her as the bus sped along. Maia checked her watch. She'd been asleep for a little over two hours. Another bump and – *crunch!* – a plastic bottle of water Maia had tucked into a side pouch of her backpack fell to the floor and rolled under Jackie's unoccupied seat. Maia felt around for it, but the bottle managed to evade her.

"Here, let me get that for you," offered the boy in the baseball cap Maia had insulted after getting on the bus.

"Thanks," Maia said, taking note of the boy's green eyes and kind, crooked smile.

"Mind if I sit a second? The kid sitting next to me is snoring like a buzz saw, and I can only get up and go to the bathroom for a break so many times before people think I ate something funny."

"Sure, no problem. My friend Jackie won't mind," Maia answered as she scooted closer to the window.

"Thanks, I appreciate it," said the boy. "Hey, when I told you before you didn't have a good poker face, I was just kidding around."

"It's okay. When I said you had bad taste in baseball teams, I meant it."

The boy laughed. "You're a firecracker – I like that. My name's Nate."

"I'm Maia."

"Nice to meet you, Maia," Nate said, extending his hand.

Maia turned slightly, reaching out to take Nate's hand. His grip was firm, but tender. A tingle crept up her arm, and Maia pulled her hand back. "You too."

"Say, are you named after the goddess? I mean that would be something considering we're in Greece."

"Um, after the star, I guess," Maia said. "My father named me. He was from Greece. So was I – that is, I was born in Greece, but I live in the U.S. with my mother on Long Island."

"Me too. My mom is in the military so we move around a lot. Right now we're in Ohio. But northern California was my favorite," Nate said, adjusting his cap.

"Is that why you're in the youth ambassador program? Do you want to work for the government like your mom?"

"Nah, my parents wanted me to do it. They think it'll look good when I apply to college. I wasn't that keen on it, but I always liked Greek history and mythology, so I was okay when I found out where I was going. What about you?"

"It was my idea," Maia answered. "I knew someone who did it a few years ago. I've been back to Greece once since I was a baby – when I was thirteen. I needed to figure out a way to make the trip again."

"Your parents didn't want to send you?"

"My dad is gone, and my mom, well, it's complicated. We don't have the money right now. My grandfather got sick a couple of years ago, and there were a lot of bills when he died," Maia said. A picture of her grandfather passed before her mind's eye – him sitting in an Adirondack chair on the front porch. He often waited there for Maia after school, always eager to hear about her day. He would've been so happy that she'd returned to Greece, Maia thought. She imagined sitting side by side with her grandfather on her front steps pretending to laugh at some bad joke he'd mangled, while drinking his favorite concoction of iced tea and lemonade.

"I'm sorry to hear that, Maia, but I'm glad for you finding a way to come back. Do you have family here?" Nate asked.

"Yeah, a lot, but just a few that I'm close to. My cousin Helena is my age, and we keep in touch. And I got close to my grandmother, but she's getting old and she never spoke much English to begin with so it's always been tough with her," Maia recounted. "Then there's my uncle, but he... he's hard to get a hold of sometimes. Anyway, hopefully I'll get to see them when we go back to Athens."

"Yeah, I've heard Athens is amazing. I really want to go to the Acropolis," Nate said, "but Olympia is pretty awesome too."

"Wait, where are we going?" Maia asked.

"All of the papers say Krestena, but we're going to be near Olympia – where the ancient Olympics started."

And Olympia was also the name some used to call the hidden world of the Greek gods, Maia recalled. She'd forgotten that Olympia was as well a town on Greece's Peloponnese peninsula.

"I read that you can run on the actual field where the ancient Greeks held their races. Say, why do you look so worried? I doubt we have to compete against the other ambassadors or anything like that."

Competition was the furthest thing from Maia's mind. When she'd first been told the name of the hidden world, she hadn't made a connection with the original site of the Olympics. But now that she thought about it, she wasn't so surprised. Maia had taught herself a lot about Greece and its mythology, but when she crossed over to Olympia her memory was somehow affected. This had troubled her then, and it was equally disconcerting now. What if she forgot something that made the difference between life and death?

Maia felt Nate's eyes on her. Sensing another remark coming about her lack of skill in hiding her emotions, Maia said, "If we do have to compete, I'm sure I can take care of myself."

"Yep, you're a real firecracker," Nate declared. "I'm going to keep an eye on you, Maia. Thanks for letting me sit awhile. I'm going back up front to deal with the buzz saw."

Nate reached out his hand to shake Maia's. As she put hers out in return, her bracelet slipped out from her long-sleeve lacrosse t-shirt.

"Hey, that's quite a sparkler you got. Is it from here?" Nate asked.

"Yeah, I got it on my last trip."

"What do the symbols mean?"

"They don't mean anything," Maia lied.

"Oh, come on now. Sure they do. Let's see. The wings mean... you're a risk taker. You like to fly."

"No, really—"

"And a sword. Well, that doesn't surprise me, 'cause you're like some warrior girl, right?" Nate continued.

Maia shifted in her seat. If possible, it was even hotter on the bus than before. "Something like that," she answered.

"I'll talk to you later, Maia."

"Okay, Nate," Maia said, not able to help herself from smiling back despite how their conversation ended.

"Excuse me," Nate said as he slid past Jackie standing in the aisle in front of him.

Jackie stared at Nate as he shuffled towards the front of the bus. Slowly she turned her head. Jackie raised her eyebrows at Maia before taking her seat.

"What's that 'look' for?"

"Isn't that—"

"The kid I made fun of before, yeah," Maia interrupted. "He's actually pretty cool. What were you talking to 'El Toro' about?"

"Who?"

"The Spanish kid – Roc."

"Oh, I don't know... lots of stuff. He's nice too."

"Jackie, did you know that we're going to Olympia?"

"I thought the town was called... hang on a second," Jackie said as she pulled a black and white marble notebook stuffed with papers from her backpack. "It's called Krestena. It says here it's very close to the 'famous site of Olympia.' Why? What's the big deal?"

"No, it's nothing. I just didn't—"

"You just didn't read the itinerary."

"I'm more of a big picture kind of person," Maia said, trying to sound disinterested. "I'm sure Krestena is a great place."

Jackie grunted affirmatively, but her eyes told a different story. "Don't expect me to remember everything. I want to have fun too." Jackie pointed at Maia's right wrist. "I heard him ask you about your bracelet."

Maia's stomach muscles stiffened. "Yeah, so what?" she said, pulling her sleeve over the bracelet.

"You never talk about it."

"Yes, I do," Maia said, sweat chilling the back of her neck.

"You don't! You're always wearing that bracelet, but you get weird anytime someone asks about it."

"Jackie, calm down. He asked me about it, but there's nothing to tell. This isn't a big deal."

"It is if you act all mysterious. You'll tell some stranger but not your best friend," Jackie said, nostrils virtually flaring.

"I didn't tell him anything, so drop it."

Jackie stuffed her notebook back into her bag and shoved it under the seat. Sitting up, she turned her back to Maia every so slightly.

"Jackie, I'm sorry."

The bus continued to hum as it sped along, but there was otherwise no sound coming from Jackie's direction.

"Can we please just forget about this?" Maia asked. "You *are* my best friend, and I'd tell you anything."

"Except about the bracelet."

"Because you're right – it's not that simple," Maia admitted as she contemplated Nate's characterization of her as a risk taker. "But I don't have to be so weird about it. Once we get to the hotel and get settled in, I'll tell you about my last trip to Greece."

"Everything?"

Maia arched her back. She could almost feel her arms strapped to a pair of makeshift wings.

"I won't leave out a single detail."

CHAPTER 7

WITHOUT FEAR

MAIA THUMBED THROUGH her youth ambassador manual as it lay perched against her pillow. Thankfully the initial meeting after they'd arrived in Krestena had been short – lots of dos and don'ts (mostly don'ts) – but it ended with a dictate that all of the youth ambassadors thoroughly review their manuals. Jackie, having read through it much quicker than Maia, had gone down the hall to the common room, presumably to continue her Spanish lessons.

"All ambassadors are expected to uphold the principles of diplomacy, dignity, and good will," Maia read aloud before closing the manual and tossing it to the floor with a thud. Rolling onto her back on the lumpy bed, Maia caught the distantly familiar scent of dried lavender and found herself back at her grandmother's house. Another lesson from her psychology class flashed through her mind. Memories could be triggered through sensory stimuli, and smells were particularly powerful. In this case, Maia recalled the fragrance of her grandmother's guest bedroom where she saw pictures of her father for the first time. Whether showing him laughing, playing, or embracing Maia and her mother, the many photographs of her father kept by her grandmother were models of domestic bliss. But they'd been taken nearly fifteen years ago, and Maia could no more remember knowing her father than she could her first day of preschool.

The clicking of a lock and key signaled Jackie's return. Maia sat up in bed just as her friend swung the door open, her expression not implying a pleasant time spent in the common room.

"That jerk! I could slap him!" Jackie shrieked.

"Who? Rocco? What did he do?"

"It's Roc! He told everyone we made out on the bus! Can you believe that? They're all going to think I'm a total—"

"Whoa, whoa, whoa," Maia interrupted. "Nobody is going to think anything. Let's go back down there and—"

"No, I can't go! I'm humiliated!" Jackie exclaimed before bursting into tears and throwing herself face down onto her bed.

After several minutes of fruitless consoling, Maia said, "Fine, stay here." She grabbed her sneakers and slipped them on as she stepped into the hallway. Jackie's muffled sobbing could still be heard after Maia closed the door and made her way down the hallway, which she didn't expect given that there'd been at least twenty noisy teenagers in the common room before she'd left to read her manual.

"Hey, Maia." It was Nate, and he was alone except for an old man sweeping the floor.

"Where is everyone?"

"Back in their rooms, I guess. One of the leaders sent everybody packing after your friend stormed out. Is she okay? I missed what happened, but she seemed pretty upset."

"Jackie's okay," Maia answered. "She thinks everybody is talking about her."

"Nah, if they're talking about anyone, it's that Spanish kid. He's getting under a lot of people's skin."

"Why aren't you back in your room?"

"I was, but I figured the coast would be clear by now," Nate replied, his eyes shifting around the room before giving Maia a sideways glance and laughing to himself.

"Breaking the rules already?"

"Do you want to play cards?" Nate asked. "Let's test out that poker face."

"Maybe later. I'm going to go for a walk," Maia said.

"Okay, suit yourself."

Maia squeezed past the old man with the broom and entered the hotel lobby. Two of the program leaders were sitting on a couch, their backs to Maia – and to the front door. She inched her way across the lobby and, with one finger at a time, pressed her hand upon the front door and pushed it open. Maia welcomed the warm rush of air and the sound of two boys chasing a girl on a bicycle. With a quick peek back at the lobby, Maia sped to the corner of the block and crossed the street. There was little time to waste.

Beads of sweat dotted Maia's forehead within minutes. During the orientation, the program leaders had stressed the importance of keeping cool in the summer heat for which Greece was known. Maia afforded their warning little attention as she strolled the streets of Krestena. While the town bore little similarity to Varkiza, her grandmother's seaside home, Maia took comfort in the sights, sounds, and smells that did bring to mind her last trip. Two old men, both with canes, were arguing as they ambled a few yards in front of her, their canes periodically flailing about. Maia stepped into the street to pass them, and in doing so nearly tripped over a dog missing large patches of hair viciously chewing on a saddle bone long stripped of any meat. Back on the sidewalk, the aroma of coffee wafted from the open door of a café. A minor tremor registered in Maia's stomach. The café was likely to have a wide variety of pastries made with honey, toasted almonds, and filo. Maia reached into her pocket and realized she'd left her wallet back in her hotel room. Better that way, Maia reasoned. She was foolish for thinking she had time to stop for sweets.

After several minutes, Maia found herself far enough away from the center of town that her stomach again began to grumble – not from hunger but from a growing trepidation. Spying a vast vacant field, Maia slipped through the grizzled rails of an old wood fence. After a few steps through the tall grass, Maia jumped back as a trio of birds exploded into flight just ahead of her. Leaning forward and resting her hands on her knees, Maia took one very long deep breath. With a groan, she pulled herself up and looked back at the road beyond the fence.

"What am I doing?" Maia mumbled. She rubbed her chin back and forth before eventually bringing both hands to her face and pressing her palms up against her eyes. In the momentary darkness, Maia pictured her mother, fraught with worry as she listened on the telephone to a program leader tell her Maia had gone missing. The last time Maia was in Greece, the circumstances that brought her into danger were largely beyond her control. But this scheme was all hers, and the blame if something went wrong would be hers as well. Sighing, Maia pulled her hands away from her face, crisscrossed her fingers, and brought back them to her chin. On her left, the sun was beginning to sink behind a grove of trees on the side of a hill. The tips of the branches took on a gentle ruddiness, like a slew of matches burning out. It seemed odd that to Maia's right another light would catch her eye, but Maia came to grips with the reality that her bracelet was glowing!

Maia shot out her arm and twisted her wrist over and over again. There was no denying that for the second time in weeks, something fantastic was happening to the bracelet. Like the rhythm of a ticking clock, the bracelet pulsated with a warm golden light. Maia brought her hand closer to her face. Despite its radiance, the bracelet remained cool. Running the fingers of her other hand over the bracelet, Maia recalled her encounter with Zeus. He hadn't told her how the bracelet worked, but then again, given her knowledge of Greek mythology, the gods weren't generally very forthcoming in their interactions with "mere mortals." Zeus had said that Maia could return to Olympia without fear if she chose to, as long as she wore the bracelet.

"That's it!" Maia exclaimed. The decision to venture to Olympia was hers to make. Zeus would keep her safe. As her resolve grew, her fear withered away until she could think of nothing else but crossing the barrier between the two worlds. Maia's eyes widened as a smile came to her lips – the bracelet grew brighter and brighter, until finally there was an unearthly flash of light.

CHAPTER 8

IN THE MIDST OF BATTLE

"FOR THE QUEEN!" a woman shouted not far away, followed by a series of screams.

Startled and unable to see, Maia fell backwards. Lying on the ground, she rubbed and blinked her eyes until her vision returned. Once the last of the orange spots disappeared from before her, Maia checked to see that her clothing had changed. And indeed, instead of her t-shirt and jeans, she was wearing a white tunic and sandals. Maia had returned to Olympia!

There was little time to rejoice or even soak in the moment as the shouting that had welcomed Maia continued to grow louder. Maia rolled onto her stomach. What was happening just beyond the small wooded area in front of her? Keeping low to the ground, Maia crept up to the trees. Between the occasional primal cries, there was a clanging noise that Maia suspected was the meeting of two metals, as well as another sound Maia recognized as the dull twang of an arrow being shot from a bow.

"Sisters, we hold this line!" yelled a woman.

Maia dashed behind a tree, standing with her back against it. Her legs quivering, she managed to poke her head around to see the source of the voice. It took Maia a moment to accept that she'd chanced to make the journey to Olympia in the midst of a battle being fought by a legion of women. They were covered in armor and brandishing swords and shields. Their opponents were men, similarly outfitted but twice in number. Arrows whizzed through the air, and Maia traced their path back to a small number of men beyond those who were bearing swords. Fearing she knew the outcome of this battle, Maia shrunk back as the men charged the women, only to see several of the men quickly cut down. One of the women in the lead swung and plunged her sword into the chests of at least four men, striking another over the head with her shield and kicking him to the ground.

"Victory will be ours, sisters!" the woman cried as she blocked a pair of arrows with her shield.

"You will lead us there, Captain Penelopeia!" another woman yelled.

Again and again, the men charged, and they were met with a ferocity that both thrilled and frightened Maia. Not all of the women were as successful as their leader, the one called Captain Penelopeia, and Maia ducked her head back behind the tree more than once as the men made some advancements.

"Where is your queen? Why does she not take to the battlefield?" asked one of the men as he held the end of his sword to a fallen woman's throat.

"Do not speak of the queen of the Amazons, fool! You are not worthy of the honor of meeting her in battle," Captain Penelopeia cried as she cut down a man in front of her before hurtling her sword into the neck of the man threatening her fellow warrior.

"Thank you, sister," said the woman on the ground. She pulled Captain Penelopeia's sword from the man's neck and handed it to her. "Let us finish them."

The captain beamed. "Yes, Skylla. They are no match for—"

"Stand aside!"

Skylla pushed Captain Penelopeia away and raised her shield, but not before an arrow struck her in the shoulder.

"Skylla, no!" Captain Penelopeia cried. "Thais! Tend to Skylla while I end this."

As one of the women rushed to Skylla's side, the captain raced towards the archer, knocking down the few remaining opponents in her path.

"You may have won today, Amazon, but my lord will—"

Captain Penelopeia didn't given the man the chance to finish, as she sliced his throat open with the edge of her shield.

"Your lord would do well to end his folly. Or he too will bleed thus."

Captain Penelopeia spotted a man stirring on the ground a few yards away and marched over to him. Kneeling, she checked him over for wounds. Seeing few injuries, the captain slapped him across the face.

"You will live, boy," Captain Penelopeia said as she pulled him to his feet. "Tell the son of Zeus that the Amazons are not to be trifled with any longer."

The man made a poor effort of swinging his fist at the captain, and she knocked him to the ground. "Let Heracles know that there shall not be further warning."

"Virago!" spat the servant of Heracles.

Captain Penelopeia kneeled and punched him in the face, rendering him unconscious. "I accept your compliment, weakling."

"Captain! Please, come!" yelled Thais.

"What is the matter? Have you pulled the arrow?" Captain Penelopeia asked as she knelt beside Skylla.

"Yes, but the arrow was tainted in poisonous aconite," Thais said in a whisper.

"Captain, tell the queen—"

"Skylla, there is nothing I will tell the queen that you cannot tell her yourself," Captain Penelopeia interrupted.

"A coin – *kaff! kaff!* – a coin for the ferryman, please," Skylla sputtered.

"Enough, sister. Charon will not ferry you today or any day soon. You will be fine. We were victorious, and the queen will… " Captain Penelopeia's voice trailed off as Skylla took her last breath. "The queen will honor you, Skylla… as will I."

The captain bowed her head and rested it atop Skylla's chest.

"I am sorry, Captain Penelopeia," offered Thais. "Is there anything I can do?"

"Yes… you can find a coin," the captain said before raising her head. "And make haste, for the queen awaits us at Olympia."

Behind the tree, Maia's legs were riddled with cramps as she tried to remain perfectly still. She cringed as Captain Penelopeia lifted Skylla and carried her across the battlefield. The other Amazons followed not far behind, gathering weapons as they made their procession. Maia looked at her bracelet. It'd stopped glowing at some point. She wondered if leaving Olympia would be as simple as willing it to happen.

Thunk!

An arrow struck the tree inches above Maia's head.

"Come out! Lay down your weapons, and your life may be spared," called one of the Amazons.

Maia froze, but her heart throbbed with such force that she feared she'd pass out.

Thunk!

A second arrow split the first. Maia rubbed her bracelet.

"Send me home!" she pleaded. "Zeus, send me home!"

The crunching of branches alerted Maia to the proximity of the approaching Amazon. She kept rubbing the bracelet, waiting for a flash of light that wouldn't come. Another snap of a branch, and Maia looked up to see who was stalking her.

"You!" the Amazon spat. "What are you doing here?"

The voice sounded familiar, but Maia didn't have the presence of mind to figure out how or why that was possible. By the grace of the gods, her bracelet began to glow. With the utterance of a final plea, Maia was met with a welcomed flash of light.

CHAPTER 9

SECRETS REVEALED

MAIA CLENCHED HER TEETH as she turned the key in the lock of her hotel room door, eager to not wake Jackie if she was asleep. The lock clicked, and Maia pushed the door open with the lightest pressure.

Creeeeeeaaaaak!

Maia raised her eyebrows expecting Jackie to react to the noise, but the room was silent except for the ceiling fan, which emitted a sound not unlike the skipping of a vinyl record. Maia stuck one foot in the room. She was wrong – there was another sound. Jackie was snoring ever so softly in her sleep. Maia added guilt to her growing list of emotional responses to the evening's proceedings. Maia stole her way into the room on tiptoe and sat on the floor with her back against the side of Jackie's bed. Her snores did little to convince Maia that her friend had drifted off peacefully, and she wondered if Jackie had cried herself to sleep. Maia pulled her knees into her chest and wrapped her arms around her legs. To say that tonight hadn't gone the way she'd hoped was a huge understatement.

Between the rhythmic clicking of the ceiling fan and Jackie's snores, Maia's eyelids began to droop, and eventually she fell asleep. It was still dark when she woke up with a stiff neck and a pain in her lower back. After an awkward stretch, Maia hobbled to the window and pulled back the corner of the curtain. The street outside was empty. A pair of mangy cats chased each other around a garbage can overflowing with fetid fish heads and other table scraps before one dashed off, leaving the victor to his spoils.

"Maia, what are you doing? What time is it?"

"Oh, Jackie, I'm sorry. I didn't mean to wake—"

"Forget it," said Jackie as she reached over and turned on a lamp. "Jeez, it's 3:12 in the morning. Did you just get in? Your bed is still made."

"I fell asleep on the floor. Jackie, it was kind of a crazy night and—"

"And you don't want to talk about it, right? No big surprise."

"I do want to talk about it. I think I have to," Maia said, her lower lip quivering.

* * *

"WHAT ARE YOU GOING to do now?" Jackie asked.

"I... I don't think I have much of a choice. I have to go back," Maia answered.

"But why? It's so dangerous!"

"No," Maia countered, "the bracelet will keep me safe."

"Yeah, that's what you said, but how did that warrior woman, um, Amazon recognize you?"

"I don't know. It seems impossible, but—"

"Call your uncle."

"What?" Maia asked. "Why would I... where did that idea come from? I told you I didn't hear back from him."

"So, call one of your other uncles."

"I can't do that."

"Or call your cousin Helena."

"Jackie, that wouldn't make sense."

"None of this makes sense, Maia, especially the fact that you want to go back. What would your mother say?"

"Please, Jackie. Don't you think I worry about that? If anything happened to me, it would kill her. But I have to believe, even after almost being struck by an arrow, that Zeus will protect me."

"You're going to do it no matter what I say, right? I don't know why you even told me," Jackie uttered.

"Because I needed to. I can't keep this all to myself anymore," Maia said. "And I'm going to need your help to sneak away. Tomorrow we're going to a museum in Olympia to meet the other delegations. Once we get there, I'm going to the *other* Olympia. You need to cover for me."

"How am I supposed to do that, Maia? I guess I just keep telling everybody you're in the bathroom?"

"I'm sure you'll come up with something better than that. Jackie, I know you think I'm crazy, but I can't let this opportunity go. One of the Amazons said they were meeting their queen at Olympia. There's a reason why I stumbled across that battle. The man who showed up in my living room said the son of Zeus was waiting for me. And it was his men that were fighting the Amazons. The queen would be on my side!"

Maia watched Jackie's face for a reaction. Seconds became minutes, but Jackie didn't move. The neon green numbers on the clock showed that they'd been talking for almost three hours. Maia stuck her head behind the curtain. The sky was red and rippled with strips of clouds, and Maia recalled a rhyme her grandfather would often repeat:

> *Red sky at night, sailors' delight.*
> *Red sky at morning, sailors take warning.*

Maia made a mental note to avoid getting on a boat as she withdrew her head and turned back to face Jackie. She still hadn't moved.

"Jackie, I know—"

"Shut up."

"Hey!"

"Just shut up, okay? I'll do it," Jackie grumbled. "Yeah, I think you're crazy, but I'm not going to try to stop you from doing this if it's so important to you."

Maia bounced over to Jackie and wrapped her arms around her. After a few seconds, Jackie hugged her back.

"Just promise me one thing," Jackie said.

"Anything," Maia said, pulling herself back to look Jackie in the eyes.

"At the first sign of trouble, you get yourself out of there. I mean it, Maia. And when you find the queen, you make sure she knows that lunatic demi-god is after you."

"I promise, Jackie," Maia said, grabbing her friend's hand. "Thank you."

"This makes that fuss with Roc last night look like nonsense, right?" Jackie asked.

"Nate said a lot of people think he's annoying."

"What's going on with you and Nate?"

"Nothing. He's just a nice guy," Maia answered as she got to her feet.

"That's it?" Jackie asked, stifling a yawn.

"Don't you think I have enough to deal with? I can't believe what time it is. We have to be ready to leave in three hours. Do you—"

"*Srrrrrnnnnnnk!*" snored Jackie.

Maia sighed. "Right. Good idea," she said before climbing into bed and forcing her eyes shut.

CHAPTER 10

A THORNY REUNION

THE SKY HAD CHANGED from red to lead-gray by the time Maia and Jackie filed onto the bus with the other delegates. Large clouds swelled above the roadway to Olympia, and what began as an innocent tapping developed into a rapid pelting of rain against the windows of the bus, so heavy that it was impossible to distinguish one drop from another. Plowing through the deluge, the bus rocked and whirred, leaving Maia, sitting alongside Jackie in the front row, with precious little quiet to orchestrate her escape from the watchful eyes of the program leaders once they reached the museum. On the other side of the road, a truck plodded through a massive puddle sending a wave of muddy water that momentarily shrouded the front windshield of the bus.

"This is insane!" Jackie cried. "We should've stayed back in the hotel."

"It's just a little rain, Jackie – nothing that the windshield wipers can't handle. Besides," Maia added, "if we'd stayed back in Krestena, I wouldn't be able to make my little side trip."

"Yeah, that would've been a real shame. Okay, okay, I'm joking. I told you, I'm going to do whatever I can to help you. Have you figured out when you're going to slip away?"

"As soon as possible," Maia answered. "I figure we're going to be mixed up with the other delegates right away, so I have to take advantage of whatever extra confusion there may be because of all this rain and duck out quickly."

"How's your bracelet?"

"Fine. Why?"

"Just wondering. Are you sure you can make the bracelet take you 'there' again?"

"I think so. I'm more worried about... " Maia trailed off.

"About what?" Jackie asked. "Maia, if you're having second—"

"No, I'm fine. I'm just wondering about that woman who seemed to recognize me. Maybe I have to do something for the bracelet to, I don't know, disguise me."

"It didn't come with instructions, I guess?"

"Ha! No, unfortunately not. And the god who gave it to me wasn't big on answering questions," Maia said.

Jackie lifted herself off the seat and looked around the bus. There wasn't anyone sitting in the rows behind or across from them.

"Who are you looking for?" Maia asked.

"Nobody, but you're talking about a *god*, and I wanted to see if anyone was close enough to hear us," Jackie answered. "You know, it's pretty amazing. That is, I'm really sorry about your dad and that kid, Icarus, but you actually flew – on your own and on a Pegasus!"

"The horse's name was Pierinos. And yes, I have to admit it's amazing. Or 'wondrous,' as Icarus used to say."

With a sputtered rumbling beneath their feet, the bus lurched to a stop. Between wipes of the rubber blades, Maia could distinguish a sign to the left of the bus. The top row was written in Greek, but underneath she read, *Archaeological Museum of Olympia*. From the middle of the bus, one of the leaders began calling out instructions, but Maia kept her eyes on the windshield.

The rain wasn't about to let up, which made it challenging to gauge the size of the museum.

"Maia," Jackie whispered with a nudge of her elbow.

"What?"

"She called your name, but you're in a different group from me. You're in a group with Nate."

Maia let her head fall back against the seat. "That's just great. He'll notice when I disappear."

The leader gave her last order, and the delegates got up in waves. With a gasp, the bus doors opened, and the driver turned sideways in his seat, drumming his fingers on his knee. The leader brushed past Maia and Jackie followed by a trickle of delegates, none of whom looked happy to be exiting the bus in the middle of a downpour.

"So, say something to him," Jackie offered. "Tell him you're sneaking off to see your cousin. I'm sure he'd cover for you."

"You'd better be right," Maia said. "Quick, give me your backpack."

"What are you going to—Hey!" Jackie cried as Maia emptied the contents of her backpack on the floor.

"Real smooth," Nate said as he edged up to Maia. "Here, let me help."

"If you really want to help me, you'll tell whoever asks that I just stepped away for a minute," Maia whispered.

"What are you talking about?" Nate asked.

"I'm meeting my cousin Helena. I'll be gone for a couple of hours and then—"

"Well, well, I guess I was on the money about you. Sure, Maia, it's no problem. But I want a full report later. Here's your cherry lip gloss."

"That's mine," Jackie said, grabbing the tube from Nate.

"Thanks, Nate. I owe you," Maia said.

"And I won't forget it," Nate said with a wink. "See you later."

Nate hopped off the bus and ran to the entrance of the museum. One of the leaders was holding the door open and waving for the delegates to hurry inside.

"This isn't going to work," Maia said. "I have to do it here."

"On the bus?"

"Once I step off, I can't just run around the building. They're watching."

"Maia, there's just a few people left on the bus. You're going to have to—"

"I know. Switch places with me," Maia said. "I'll go as soon as you get up."

"Isn't the driver going to notice? There's always a flash of light," Jackie said.

"Distract him."

"How?" Jackie asked.

"I don't know. Tell him what a good job he did driving in the rain," Maia suggested.

"Oh, boy. Okay, fine," Jackie said, grabbing Maia's hand. "Good luck!"

Jackie stood up after the last of the delegates passed by. Maia kneeled down as Jackie stepped into the aisle.

"I'm the last one," Jackie said to the driver.

"That is good. I need to use the bathroom. Go!" the driver barked in return.

"Oh, okay," Jackie said, stepping off the bus followed by the driver. With another gasp of stale air, the doors closed.

"Well, that couldn't have gone better if I *had* planned it," Maia mumbled to herself. Without any distractions other than the rain pegging the windows, she put her mind to triggering the bracelet.

Maia smirked as she recalled Jackie's comment about a lack of instructions.

"Okay, so how about this? *By the powers vested... in this bracelet... by Lord Zeus... take me to Olympia!*" Not surprisingly, nothing happened. Maia shifted her legs and her bottom landed on the floor of the bus. She shook her wrist and leered at the bracelet. For a moment, it seemed to glow, but just as quickly it stopped.

"Come on, this seemed so easy yesterday," Maia griped. Outside the bus, Maia heard what sounded like arguing. Peeking out past the back of the driver's seat, Maia heard one of the voices get louder. The driver was trudging back to the bus! Maia closed her eyes and tried to picture herself in Olympia. With nothing to show for her efforts, Maia backed herself as far into the row as possible while the driver opened the doors and stomped aboard. With a string of what Maia presumed were curses and a turn of the ignition, the driver threw the bus in reverse.

Crouched on the floor, Maia kept her eyes closed, scenes of Olympia passing through her mind like a slideshow. One memory in particular caught her attention – the cruel, spoiled princess Akantha, her heart broken by Icarus's rejection of her, sprawled out on the ground after meeting with a wooden plank Maia was holding. Maia didn't need to open her eyes to know that the bracelet was glowing. For a second, Maia felt nothing beneath her, but then the empty space was filled. Like the treacherous girl in the memory that focused her attention well enough to activate the bracelet, Maia was greeted by mud. She'd fallen from what would've been the height of the floor of the bus.

"*Oof!*" Maia heaved as she sat up. Her backside ached worse than from the spill she'd taken when her grandfather had overdone waxing the hallway outside of her bedroom. Maia stretched and rolled over onto her hands and knees. "I've got to remember that little snag when I cross over," she mumbled. Getting to her feet, Maia surveyed her surroundings. The mud puddle was one of many in a field with several lonely patches of discolored grass. Maia's eyes followed a pair of narrow tracks she assumed were left by a wagon or chariot through the muddy field to a grove of trees. Maia took a single step when an arrow whizzed by her left ear. Turning around, she locked eyes with a young woman adorned in armor. She was no taller than Maia herself.

"The gods must desire this reunion," the young woman said, skipping towards Maia in a manner that seemed to conflict with her attire. "What else could explain my good fortune?"

"What do you want with me?" Maia asked. "Who are you?"

"Do you not remember me? How insulting! But it matters not," the young woman said, raising her bow. "You may know me as your escort to the Underworld."

Maia crouched down, set to dive out of the path of the arrow once loosed. The young woman flashed her teeth as she pulled back the bowstring and released – only to have the arrow splintered apart by a large, whirling projectile that hummed as it cut its way through the air. Hitting the ground, the object was shown to be a shield, and Maia silently thanked its bearer for saving her. The young woman cursed as she reached for another arrow from her quiver.

"Lower your weapon, Akantha!" ordered a woman from behind Maia.

"Akantha?" Maia repeated, looking the young woman over. "Is that really... what happened to you?"

"Captain Penelopeia, allow me this kill. Please, I beg of you!" Akantha exclaimed, paying Maia no attention. "I do not know how she has come here, but you must know she is the one that caused my father's death!"

"Amazons do not kill the defenseless, especially not one of our own," Captain Penelopeia said. "Bring me my shield."

"But captain!"

"Enough! We bring her to the queen. Let her hear your charges."

Akantha stormed forward and grabbed Maia by the arm. "I shall have your blood on my arrows yet. The queen will allow it once she knows who you are."

"Akantha, that is enough!" Captain Penelopeia said. "Do not speak for the queen. Give her to me."

The captain took Maia by the shoulders. "There now, you do not look so fearsome."

"She is, Captain Penelopeia! I tell you, I know her!"

"Then what is her name?"

"I do not remember," Akantha admitted.

"You do not remember? You claim that she brought down your father's kingdom, but you do not know her name?" Captain Penelopeia asked.

"Please, captain! I must—"

"Enough! Leave us, Akantha, before you anger me further. Return to the campsite," Captain Penelopeia commanded. "I will join you there shortly."

"Yes, my captain," Akantha said. She picked up Captain Penelopeia's shield and wiped it clean of mud before offering it. With a furtive glance at Maia, Akantha bowed and dashed off in the direction of the trees.

"Th-thank you," Maia said, her voice and hands trembling far more than she wished.

"Do not thank me yet, Maia," Captain Penelopeia answered. "You must still go before the queen."

"How do you know my name?" Maia asked.

"Because I suspect I knew the man who gave it to you."

CHAPTER 11

A CHILLING SCREAM

MAIA SAID NOTHING all the while she followed Captain Penelopeia to the campsite of the Amazons. The captain's claim to knowing her father was even more troubling than nearly being struck down by someone she'd never expected to see again. Akantha was an Amazon?

Maia's puzzlement made it more of a struggle to keep pace with Captain Penelopeia, whose stride reflected a confidence Maia both admired and feared. Climbing the last of numerous hills, Maia's foot caught on a tree root poking up from the ground and tumbled forward. But before she smacked the earth, Captain Penelopeia grabbed her and put her back on her feet.

"Thanks," Maia muttered.

The captain looked at Maia with a crinkly brow. "I said not to thank me."

"I'm sorry."

"And do not say you are sorry," scolded Captain Penelopeia. "I will not tolerate weakness, not from one of your lineage. Now, watch where you step."

Cresting the hill, Maia felt a stabbing pain in her ankle, but the thought of complaining barely registered as she endeavored to not fall behind. Still, the captain had mentioned her father again, which encouraged Maia to attempt to gather some information.

"Excuse me, but how did you know my father?" Maia asked.

"He was an ally to the Amazons. That is all I will tell you. The rest is up to the queen if she sees fit."

"But you did know him?"

"I believe I made it clear that I did," Captain Penelopeia answered.

"I never knew him," Maia stated.

Captain Penelopeia stopped and Maia nearly plowed into her – an act that Maia was sure would make her look even weaker in the captain's eyes.

"You may not have known your father, but those of us who did hold him in the highest of regards. You should be proud."

"I would be if I knew anything about him," Maia responded.

Captain Penelopeia looked as though she might speak, but she was diverted by a cry that came from the ether. Several yards ahead of them, an Amazon appeared to step out from behind a large object, though the field was free of landmarks.

"Captain! The queen cries for you!" called the Amazon.

"Follow me," Captain Penelopeia yelled as she ran towards the Amazon. "Allow the girl entry."

Maia did her best to keep up. As Captain Penelopeia passed the other Amazon, who remained with her arm out as if to hold open a door, she disappeared. Maia stopped running and stared at the space into which the captain had charged.

"This way, you fool," the Amazon said.

Maia continued to gape before taking one tentative step and then another, until finally she passed by the Amazon. Instead of an empty field, Maia stood in a bustling campsite, her senses roused by the clanging of swords, the forging of horseshoes, and the rushing of scores of women young and old in various forms of dress.

"Move," the Amazon said, prodding Maia towards a tent. "You will await the return of the captain here."

A chilling scream cut through the thick smoky air of the campsite. The Amazons stopped their activities and looked in the direction of a large tent apart from the others. Maia followed suit, and her interest was met with a succession of equally terrifying cries.

"The queen is in much pain," said the Amazon, pushing Maia. "This is a mournful day for our people. Now, go! And do not wander."

But Maia could scarcely move. On more than one occasion, she'd accompanied her mother to work at the hospital. Once, she'd waited for her mother on a bench outside the emergency room as the survivors from a multi-car accident were rushed in for desperately needed medical attention. The agonizing cries of a young girl injured in the accident haunted Maia for weeks afterwards, but they were nothing compared to the suffering emanating from the queen's tent. What could've caused the leader of a powerful tribe of warrior women to be in such pain?

Maia felt the slightest tinge of pain just below her chin. The blade of a sword grazed the skin, creating a sensation not unlike that of a paper cut. Maia took several quick, deep breaths, the intensity of the sound of each progressive exhalation filling her ears and blocking the cries of the queen.

"Make no sound," Akantha whispered from behind Maia. "I will not hesitate to kill you. Get into the tent."

Akantha reached an arm around Maia and wrenched open the triangular tent flap before pushing Maia inside. Maia fell to her knees. Flipping over to a crouching position on her hands and bottom, Maia moved to leap at her captor, but Akantha stuck the sword at Maia's throat before any attempt of escape could be made. Akantha made a clucking sound with her mouth as she tapped Maia's chin with the sword. A smile like that of a demented clown from a horror movie crossed her face, and the clucking sound changed to a tittering that chilled Maia's spine.

"Long have I dreamt of this moment. Three years it has been," Akantha hissed, "three years since you destroyed everything I held precious. Oh, how I have longed to see that look in your eyes, knowing that your bold winged escape – your attempt to defy your fate – was all for naught."

From outside, the queen gave a long, excruciating scream that caused Akantha to look away. Maia rolled backwards and kicked up her legs, knocking the sword from Akantha's hands. Growling, Akantha dove on top of Maia, and the two tussled around on the ground like a pair of lionesses competing for the same carcass. Despite her best efforts, Maia ultimately lied pinned with Akantha, her knee to Maia's throat, sneering above her.

"That was futile. I am an Amazon. The spoiled, whimpering princess you knew is long gone," Akantha said as she reached back and picked up her sword. "Still, I shall have my revenge for what you did."

Akantha stood, and Maia rolled onto her side, free to cough once her throat was no longer being compressed under Akantha's weight.

"What did I do to you? Your father had me kidnapped! Icarus helped me escape. I didn't cause—"

"Enough! I do not care to hear your protests. And do not mention the artificer's son. My sword will rest in his heart soon enough," Akantha countered.

"Icarus is dead, Akantha. He fell into the sea. Icarus never made it to the mainland with me," Maia said, her cheeks reddening.

"And? You are beyond naïve if you think that his story ends there."

"What is that supposed to mean?" Maia asked.

"I will not speak any further about that fool. I shrink at the thought of my own childish affections for him. No, let us speak of my father instead. After your 'valiant escape,' we lost everything. Lord Zeus had already discarded him. It did not take long for our kingdom to fall to ruin." Akantha paused, a single tear rolling down her cheek. "My father leapt to his death from the very cliff from which you took flight. I was left with nothing."

"Akantha, if you're looking for me to apologize, it's not going to happen. Your father was going to have me killed. Don't expect me to be sorry about any of this," Maia said.

"You are bold. I will grant you that. But it matters not whether you beg for mercy or lie there defiant until your final breath," Akantha said, gripping her sword. "Captain Penelopeia will certainly not approve, but sadly for you she is too preoccupied with the queen's health to care much about your fate."

"The captain said she knew my father. I think I'm more important to her than you're letting on."

"Your father? You dare speak of your father after I told you how you caused the death of my own. I am not so impressed by your father, even if he was—"

The flap of the tent flew open and in stormed the Amazon who'd ordered Maia to wait. "What do you think you are doing, Akantha?" she asked, knocking the sword from Akantha's hands.

"Bremusa, leave us be. My business with this whelp does not concern you," Akantha said.

"Are you forgetting your place, Akantha?" Bremusa asked, a flicker of anger in her words. "You are no longer a princess. You have no business apart from that of being loyal to our queen."

Bremusa grabbed Maia by the upper arm and pulled her to her feet. "You are to come with me."

"Where are you taking her?" Akantha shrilled.

"To the queen, by order of Captain Penelopeia. You should be grateful, Akantha, that I stopped you when I did. The captain would have just as soon cast you out if you had harmed her."

"Cast me out!" Akantha shouted. "As long as my father's killer lives, I will find no peace here."

"Peace? Akantha, how you disappoint me," Bremusa said. "You were near death when we found you. The queen took you in, nursed you back to health, and gave you a new life as an Amazon. You have fought by my side, and I came to know you as a sister, as did the others. But I was mistaken it seems. The queen suffers terribly. And we have the son of Zeus plaguing us, looking to end our people. There is no peace at hand. If your heart so differs from mine, then you should go."

Akantha stared at the dirt floor of the tent while Bremusa spoke, her whole body quivering. With a snort, Akantha picked up her sword and pushed past Bremusa and Maia, exiting the tent. Maia's knees buckled. Fighting a dizzy spell, her eyes fell upon her bracelet. Maia's knuckles turned white as she made a fist. By no means had Zeus kept his promise of unrecognizability. And for Akantha of all people to single her out! As her thoughts shifted to the crazed look on the dethroned princess's face while she ranted about Icarus, Maia felt a great tug on her arm.

"Come," Bremusa said, "the queen awaits."

CHAPTER 12

THE BROKEN SPEAR

MAIA STEPPED OUT OF THE TENT with Bremusa close behind her. The campsite had grown quiet, but the air remained filled with scents that were as foreign to Maia as the clothes she wore. She filled her nostrils with air tinged with herbs and a metallic smoke that made Maia crinkle her nose. An Amazon on horseback trod over to them and dismounted, landing in a puddle that splashed mud on Maia's feet and legs.

"Marpe, praise the gods you have returned safely," said Bremusa. "How was your scouting mission?"

"It was fruitless. But what has happened in my absence? Our sisters are in a state of terrible distress," Marpe responded. "Is the queen—"

"No, Marpe, the queen suffers greatly from her injury, but she lives."

"And yet we do nothing?" Marpe asked. "Heracles has killed how many of our number, and we remain in hiding? This is not the way of the Amazons."

"What is our way, Marpe? Since the war on Mount Olympus, our path is no more certain than that of a butterfly in a tempest. Stand aside. I must bring this girl to the queen."

"Her? What right does she have to deserve an audience with our queen if she suffers so?" Marpe asked.

"I follow Captain Penelopeia's orders."

"And you do so blindly, Bremusa. That has always been your weakness," Marpe uttered before pulling herself back onto her horse and spurring the animal to charge off.

"Why does the captain want me to go to the queen?" Maia asked as Bremusa goaded her forward.

"Do not ask questions," Bremusa ordered. "We have wasted enough time already."

For a group of women that referred to each other as sisters, Maia noted a less than affectionate manner of interacting. Still, even if her last brush with the royalty of Olympia had been perilous at best, she was safer among the Amazons – with the obvious exception of Akantha – than on her own. And there was their common enemy as well. The threat of Heracles, the son of Zeus, loomed outside the fantastic field that protected the campsite from view.

Approaching the queen's tent, Maia couldn't begin to imagine how anyone could get past the dragon-like guard, quite possibly with fire-breathing ability at her disposal, towering over the opening. In a flash, the guard thrust a spear inches from Maia's nose. Staring at the tip of the spear, Maia let out a short squeak that she immediately wished she could take back. The guard retracted the spear an inch upon seeing Bremusa.

"The girl is to see the queen. And I dare say, her highness could not ask for a more stalwart protector than you," Bremusa said.

"I would die for the queen," the guard grunted, "and kill as well, of course."

Maia continued to stare at the tip, not failing to note the guard's threat against her. Through the corner of her eye, she looked to Bremusa for hope that she would be allowed to pass the dragon.

"You honor the queen. But trust in me that this girl will do her no harm. Let us pass."

The guard stiffened, bringing the spear back to her side. In doing so, she let out a noise that reminded Maia of a particularly tough lacrosse teammate who'd earned the nickname "Bulldog" for the litany of growls and grumbles that came forth from her during a game. Her head bowed, Maia raised the corners of her mouth to offer a smile in gratitude for not being stabbed, but the guard stared past her, as if something of interest was happening over Maia's shoulders.

Bremusa grabbed Maia's elbow and pulled her into the tent. Maia shuddered at the smell that inundated her nostrils. Gagging and sputtering, Maia turned her head back to the opening of the tent, trying to draw in the outside air. Grabbing Maia by the hair, Bremusa pulled the flap closed.

"That is enough!" Bremusa ordered. "Do not carry on this way in front of the queen."

"But the smell—"

"Quiet!"

Maia rubbed her watering eyes. Blinking, she flinched at the scene before her. Captain Penelopeia watched over a woman lying on a bed of pillows. The woman's arms and legs twitched, and her face was contorted with pain. After several quick, short breaths, the woman let out an agonizing scream that cut through the air and vibrated the walls of the tent.

"What has happened, Captain Penelopeia?" Bremusa asked.

"They attempted to remove the spearhead," answered the captain. "And they succeeded in causing Queen Hippolyta greater pain."

The queen let out a run of moans, each louder than the one before, until finally she lay her head down with her mouth agape and her eyes rolled back. No other sounds came forth.

"Thais, this was folly," said Captain Penelopeia to the Amazon kneeling beside the queen. "You are no closer to a remedy than when the son of Zeus first struck."

"What would you have me do, captain?" asked Thais. "The wound is getting worse. Trying to remove the spearhead again seemed our sole recourse."

"This is dark enchantment indeed," said Bremusa, her voice wavering. "Captain Penelopeia, I have brought the girl."

"Come forward," the captain ordered.

"And you call my actions 'folly'?" Thais mocked. "What purpose could this girl serve other than to bring parasites into this sacred place?"

With a push from Bremusa, Maia dragged her feet until she reached Captain Penelopeia's side.

"I don't—"

"Take hold of the spearhead," Captain Penelopeia said to Maia.

"Are you mad? I cannot allow you to—"

Before Thais could continue, the captain drew her sword and brought it dangerously close to her neck.

"Captain, stop!" shouted Bremusa. "We cannot allow ourselves to give into recklessness. Thais is doing all that she can to heal the queen. This girl should not be allowed to go any farther."

"Bremusa, I thank you for your counsel, but I am certain of the outcome. Whatever gods remain on Mount Olympus favored us today. They sent this girl. It can be no coincidence. Now, take hold of the spearhead."

Maia clenched her fists until her fingers turned a vivid crimson. She dared not move, even with Captain Penelopeia standing next to her, radiating a level of potential hurt that caused Maia to drip with sweat from her brow. She felt a hand wrap around the back of her neck, and she turned to look up into the captain's eyes.

"Do not oblige me to tell you again. Take hold of the spearhead!"

Maia opened her right hand, followed by her left. She cupped them together and brought them to her mouth. After a moment and a tightening of the grip on her neck, Maia reached forward and put her right hand on the spearhead. It burned, but Maia wrapped her fingers around the wrecked weapon sticking out of the queen's side.

"Now what?" Maia asked.

"Pull."

Moaning, the queen began to quake, and Maia wrenched the spearhead with such force that she fell backward onto the ground. Sitting up, Maia realized she was still holding the spearhead and threw it aside. Her hand was soiled with blood. Maia wiped it across her tunic until there was little trace of it.

"The girl did it!" Bremusa cried.

"How did you know, Captain Penelopeia?" Thais asked.

"If you knew her father, you would scarcely be surprised," answered the captain. "But even I did not expect that!"

Captain Penelopeia pointed at the queen's side. With the spearhead gone, the wound was closing and the skin surrounding it turning color from maroon to a healthy pink. The queen stirred, and she opened her eyes as the wound disappeared.

"Queen Hippolyta! Praise Olympus that you live!" cried Thais, falling to her knees.

Captain Penelopeia pulled Maia to her feet and pointed to a spot near the opening of the tent. Maia obeyed and retreated to the corner.

The captain drew closer to the queen, placing her hand on Thais's shoulder, whose sobs made it difficult to hear anything else. Thais rose and moved aside, allowing Captain Penelopeia to take to her knees close to the queen.

"My queen, we await your commands."

Queen Hippolyta reached out and put her palm on the hilt of the captain's sword.

"Then to arms, sisters. The son of Zeus has his reckoning at hand," Queen Hippolyta vowed.

CHAPTER 13

CHAOS REIGNS

JERKED FROM HER CORNER, Maia was rushed out of the queen's tent and carelessly flung aside as news of the queen's recovery spread throughout the campsite. Cries of joy abounded, and Maia felt a swelling of pride (or was it adrenaline?) at having saved the queen. But how had she done it? The healers hadn't been able to remove the spearhead. From the way they spoke, she doubted that even the queen's mammoth guard ("Bulldog") could have managed it. As more and more Amazons rushed the tent, Maia was nudged farther and farther from the queen's dwelling, until she was at a reasonable distance to slip away unnoticed. Maia's eyes wandered to her bracelet. It was time to go home.

Some of the Amazons began chanting, their words muffled by the whoops and cries of their sisters. Maia edged her way around the tent. Free from watch, she crouched down and closed her eyes. Maia thought about Zeus's words, willing the bracelet to be triggered. Seconds passed, and she pried open one eye. The bracelet was glowing no more than any other part of her body. Clenching her eyes closed, Maia searched her memory for anything that would spark an emotional response. The image of a gryphon was taking shape in her mind's eye when she found herself knocked off her feet. The hideous beast faded away from sight, replaced by a sullen but equally intimidating Captain Penelopeia.

"You disappoint me by sneaking away like a student of Autolycus," the captain scolded.

"I didn't *sneak* anywhere. I was pushed away," Maia answered, brushing dirt from her hands and knees.

"Stand up."

"Okay, but let's get one thing straight here. I didn't do anything wrong, and you're all treating me like garbage. I'm so out of here," Maia said.

"You saved the queen."

"Yeah, how about that? I saved your queen, and you thank me by knocking me on my ass. I guess the next—"

Before she could finish, Captain Penelopeia kneeled before Maia, as she did moments ago in front of the queen. The sight of the mighty warrior so humbled nearly caused Maia to fall to the ground again.

"The Amazons are forever in your debt. I beseech you to grant me the honor to escort you to your chosen destination," Captain Penelopeia said.

"Um, it's okay. I don't need an escort. I just need—"

"The bracelet. It was a gift from Mount Olympus?" the captain asked, rising to her feet.

"Yes... from Zeus. He gave it to me for my protection. It's supposed to do other things too, but it's not working right."

"The king of the gods is dead. For that reason the bracelet would seem to fail you."

"How could... what do you mean 'dead'? He's one of the gods. They're immortal!"

"Lord Zeus is dead, I assure you. Perhaps you or I would have failed to execute the almighty wielder of the thunderbolt, but his brethren were more than capable," Captain Penelopeia said. She pulled her sword from her belt and pitched it into the ground. The captain rested her hands atop the hilt, dropping her shoulders. "We all pay the price."

"But he said he would protect me. He said... " Maia's words trailed off as she grasped how truly vulnerable she was – and how foolish she was to have come back to this place.

"Mount Olympus is in ruins. The gods who survive are so weakened that they may as well be dead. Chaos reigns over Olympia."

"The war," Maia mouthed. She squeezed her eyes shut and drew a long, exaggerated breath.

"What are you saying?"

Opening her eyes, Maia replied, "There was talk of a war between the gods the last time I was here. It sounded like everyone was being dramatic, but I guess you're telling me it finally happened?" Ready to rip it off her wrist, Maia gripped her bracelet until she could feel the symbols of the wings and sword pressing into her.

"Do not take it off. There appears to be some of Lord Zeus's enchantment in the bracelet yet, and you may still have need of it. To answer your distressing question, yes, there was a war. You seem to know of its origins, and indeed your aforementioned visit accelerated its occurrence."

"Wait a minute. Are you saying I'm to blame?"

"I said nothing about blame, child. You cannot be held responsible for the circumstances of your birth. Nor would I blame your father, though it was his exodus from Olympia that gave voice to those that ultimately challenged the authority of Lord Zeus."

"My father?"

"Yes. He was of considerable—"

"Just stop, okay. I'm so sick of hearing you people talk about my father when no one will ever be honest with me about him. He's a total stranger to me, but somehow you and others, like that deranged princess, Akantha, seem to know a lot about him," Maia yelled.

Captain Penelopeia narrowed her eyes to slits. She leaned into her sword, pushing it another inch into the ground. In a flash, the Amazon grabbed the sword and raised it to Maia's chin, shooting mud across her face.

"Ugh! What the hell was that for?"

Ignoring her question, the captain glared at Maia. Returning her gaze, Maia said, "Whatever you're going to do, just get it over with."

Captain Penelopeia continued to stare, and then with an almost imperceptible smile lowered her sword. "He went by many names. But I believe there is someone who wishes to tell you the rest."

"Who?" Maia asked.

"I shall, Maia," said Queen Hippolyta, emerging from behind the corner of the tent. "It is the very least I could do for rescuing me from the realm of Hades. Captain Penelopeia, my most faithful sister, your warriors await direction. Will you ask Bremusa to see that we are not bothered?"

"Of course, my queen," the captain said with a bow.

"Thank you. Come, Maia. There is much for us to discuss."

"But you were hurt," Maia sputtered. "You should be resting and not wasting your time with me."

Queen Hippolyta looked warmly upon Maia. "Your concern for my health is touching, as is your self-deprecation. But despair not, for I am no longer in danger. You saw to my safety by removing the spearhead."

"Yeah, how exactly was I able to do that?"

"One of many questions I pledge to answer, Maia, before this day is through."

INTERLUDE I

TWO DAYS BEFORE THE CREATION OF OLYMPIA

LORD ZEUS, FATHER AND KING of gods and men, clasped his son's hand. The fingers were dried and twisted, and the gray skin emanated the cold of space – so contrasting to the warmth the god of the sun had generated in life. But nothing made sense anymore. The Great War had changed everything, even atop Mount Olympus, where change had always come at a ruinous cost.

Above Zeus, the sky erupted in a blaze of lightning and flames that shook the heavens themselves. A gust of wind coiled through the columns marking the edge of the sanctuary of Zeus and rushed past the king of the gods. Lifting his head, Zeus closed his eyes, and (for a moment) a tear appeared to trickle along his cheek. As quickly as it had come, the wind subsided, and the sky quieted to a murky purple speckled with lackluster stars. Zeus maintained his vigil until interrupted by a voice cutting through the fleeting silence.

"My lord, how do you hide away when there is so much—but what has happened to fair Apollo?" asked Hera, wife of Zeus and queen of the gods of Olympus. "His stillness causes me a fright I have never known."

"'Stillness,' you say? Indeed, you have every reason to be afraid. The son of Zeus is dead, Hera," Zeus boomed. "Your folly has extinguished his light, and there is nothing that can be done."

"No, my husband! This is not possible! Apollo is a god. He can no more die than you or I," Hera declared, a pitch to her voice that seemed to slice through the mists enveloping Mount Olympus. "Wake him!"

"Were that but our circumstances, my imprudent wife," Zeus said, laying Apollo's hand to rest upon his lifeless chest. "Your interference in the affairs of man has left the world in ruins. Man's faith is lost. The gods are doomed."

"My lord, how can you make such pronouncements? If the mortals have lost their way, as you say, and dare question our absolute sovereignty, then it is our obligation to win them back! You must—"

"Silence! You are in no position to make demands of the king of the gods," Zeus roared, his voice trailed by the crackling of lightning in the sky above. "Lord Zeus ordered you all to stand down, but you continued to meddle despite my mandate. You, my most traitorous wife, and my reckless brother Poseidon above all hold the greatest share of the blame... and the responsibility for our most calamitous circumstances."

"This is madness! Were we to allow the Achaeans to fall? How many of our children were to perish against the forces of Troy? No, my lord, we were right to enter the battle. Had Poseidon's cries of war not awoken you from your slumber—"

CRACK-OW!

"Lord Zeus slept because of your treachery!"

"Had you not been awoken," Hera continued, "there would have been far fewer fatalities for the Achaeans. Though ultimately vanquished, the Trojans had made too far an advancement. No, my husband, I do not regret my actions, nor would I condemn Poseidon. It was your lack of engagement that cost the gods the faith of the Achaeans."

"This was a war to be fought between men, not immortals!" boomed Zeus. "You are wife to the king of the gods, but you are not meant to understand all matters under the purview of your husband."

"Enough of your spiteful reproach. We waste precious time with this empty dialogue. Come, my husband. We will remind the Achaeans of our eminence," pleaded Hera.

"Look upon Apollo. It is too late. Nonetheless, you are correct in that Lord Zeus will debate this no further."

"My lord, you have conceded defeat, but I will not. Mount Olympus will stand, more stunning in its glory than ever," said Hera.

"Reach out to them then. Call upon your most steadfast followers," Zeus commanded. "Then tell Lord Zeus that the fate of Mount Olympus is secure."

Hera closed her eyes. Within moments, she shuddered. Her face exposing a clash of excruciating sensations, Hera gasped and fell to her knees. She brought her hands up, and in doing so clutched her face as she unleashed a cry filled with pain never before experienced by a god of Olympus. "No... no, it is intolerable!"

"Heed the words of Lord Zeus and grant that there is no further reason for dispute. "

"Still, my lord, what cruelty is this? My hands are more blue than the waters of Sounion and colder than the very depths of Tartarus," wailed Hera. "The Achaeans... they did refuse my grace!"

"Their faith in the wife of Lord Zeus has weakened to a state where your every path will lead you to rest at Apollo's side," said Zeus. "And in time, Mount Olympus will founder."

"Can there not be a remedy?"

"Not one without sacrifice, my ill-fated wife," answered Zeus.

"Then I shall be the one to make it. Please, my lord, tell me what can be done!"

"We must leave this place. We must gather the most fervent of our followers while they remain so and depart this realm for another," Zeus declared. "There is no other way."

"And the sacrifice?"

"It will be yours and Poseidon's to make. For the remaining Olympians to last, you will vacate your stations and live amongst the mortals. The release of your godly forces will allow us to create a new world."

"That is too much! You would have your wife and brother renounce their thrones?" Hera shrilled. "You spoke of sacrifice, but this is deicide."

"Poseidon has already acquiesced."

"Such lunacy! The seas must have their god."

"His son Triton is more than able to take his place," said Zeus. "And as for you, wife, your throne will stay empty. That is the most Lord Zeus can promise."

"And where would you have your wife go?"

"Do not presume that Lord Zeus is pleased with this. Were there another way, he would consider it. If we do not act soon, more of the Achaeans will abandon us. You may complain about your lot, but you will live, unlike Apollo."

"But as a mortal. What manner of life would you have me suffer?" asked Hera. "No, let another make the sacrifice."

"Do not dare to attempt to relieve yourself of your liability. It is decided," declared Zeus. "We take Poseidon and make our journey to the garden of the Hesperides."

"But what need do we have of the nymphs of the West?"

"No need at all," Zeus answered, reaching a hand to the sky. With a deafening clap, a thunderbolt materialized in his hands.

"Lord Zeus will have an audience with their father. The time has come for him to lay down his burden."

CHAPTER 14

QUEEN OF THE AMAZONS

"LET ME SEE YOUR BRACELET," Queen Hippolyta said. Maia wiped her hand repeatedly across the front of her tunic, dirt blending in with the queen's dried blood, before bearing her right arm. Her fingers wiggled like worms left out in the sun. Queen Hippolyta pressed her hand into Maia's. It felt as soft as a satin glove, but powerful too – when Queen Hippolyta turned Maia's wrist, she felt the grip of someone she would fear in battle. After a few turns of the bracelet, the queen released Maia's hand. She held it out for a moment before making a fist and crossing her arms in front of her chest.

"A gift from Lord Zeus," Queen Hippolyta stated. "Crafted by fire in the workshop of Hephaestus, no doubt. It is beautiful, though no longer possessing the power it once did. The wings symbolize—"

"Icarus... from the last time I was here," Maia said, the face of Daedalus's son in the moment before he fell to the sea flashing in front of her eyes. "There were a lot more when Zeus gave it to me. All but the wings disappeared right afterward."

"And the sword?"

"That showed up before I came back here. I don't know what it means or how it got there. But if the wings are for my incident with Icarus, then the sword must be for something that's happening now," Maia proposed.

"Your 'incident' with Icarus was quite eventful for the denizens of Olympia," said Queen Hippolyta. "As it turned out, it led to the toppling of Mount Olympus. Now wait, child. I can see from your face that you took that to mean some form of responsibility on your part. That is not what I meant. Come and sit next to me."

Queen Hippolyta laid down her staff and sat upon the grass-covered ground. Closing her eyes, she ran her fingers through the blades of sweet onion grass as though she were rubbing a newborn kitten's fur. "*Hmmm*. It is not often that the queen of the Amazons is granted the opportunity to feel Gaia's adornments." The queen's eyes popped open. "Especially not with recent events."

"You have to, uh, stop and smell the roses."

"What is that, child?"

"Oh," Maia answered, "it's just an expression where I come from."

"*Hmmm*. And a good edict it is at that. Though, as our goddess of beauty and love, Aphrodite, once learned in Cyprus, where there is a rose, there is also a thorn. Would you agree?"

"I, uh, I guess so," Maia said, wishing she'd kept her sayings to herself.

"What else do they say in your world?"

"About roses?" Maia asked.

"No, not more about roses. There are rumors... stories about your meeting on the isle of Alphaios. They say you were questioned by a council about the rejoining."

"Yes, I was. I told them I didn't think the people of my world would like it. I'm not sure that was the answer King Alphaios was hoping I'd give," Maia said with a trifle of a laugh.

"No, I would think not. Alphaios was more in favor of the rejoining than most others. It was, as some say, an obsession that ultimately led to his downfall," Queen Hippolyta told.

"Did you know him well?"

"Well enough. Ha! Well enough to know what a small-minded man he was. Alphaios was hardly a great thinker. He had Daedalus in his ear for an eternity until they had a falling out. I dare say, what are you laughing at?"

"Oh, I'm sorry. It's just that you're, well, you're not like I expected," Maia sputtered.

"And what false expectation did you have of the queen of the Amazons?"

"No, it wasn't anything bad. I wasn't thinking specifically about you. The only other royalty I've met were King Alphaios... and his psychotic daughter," said Maia.

"Akantha. Yes, well, I will take your laughter as a compliment then. Though Akantha has proven herself to be a rather worthy Amazon," Queen Hippolyta offered.

"She threatened to kill me when Captain Penelopeia first brought me to camp."

"Then again, she is likely as thick as was her father."

Maia bit her lip to keep from laughing. Queen Hippolyta's sense of humor was a welcome surprise.

Queen Hippolyta grinned. "Oh, you can laugh, child. Perhaps some levity is needed after coming so close to making passage on Charon's boat. I will see to Akantha. She will trouble you no more. Now, as I began, you are no more responsible for the fall of Mount Olympus – or Alphaios's cowardly expiration – than I am for the insanity of Heracles. It was folly on the part of Lord Zeus to believe the creation of Olympia would secure his and his family's existence. After the Great War, nothing could have prevented their demise."

"But it worked for a while, right? It's been centuries. That's longer than the gods probably would've survived," Maia said.

"Centuries matter not in the lifespan of a god. Nay, as time does pass in Olympia, the Great War may have occurred mere days ago."

"I don't understand."

"It is no matter," Queen Hippolyta said. "Tell me, child. What forms do you see when you look at Lord Zeus's clouds?"

"Oh, I'm horrible at that. All I ever see is big cotton balls," Maia replied.

"That is terribly disappointing. Look there. I see an amphisbaena."

"You see a what?"

"Ugh, an amphisbaena – a serpent with two heads. Look!" Queen Hippolyta commanded.

"Oh, yeah, now I see it."

"You are an awful liar."

Maia scrunched her toes in her sandals. "I told you, I'm not good at that. My mother always asks me what I see too, but it's the same when I look at the stars. I can never see the 'Big Dipper' or 'Orion's belt' or whatever constellation everybody else sees. They just look like stars. And those clouds just look like marshmallows."

"I fear I do not know what *marshmallows* are, but I doubt they are as much a threat as an amphisbaena."

"They're good with chocolate and graham crackers," Maia offered.

"*Hmmm.* Perhaps we should speak about your father."

"Yes!"

"He was a good man, and Lord Zeus knows those are few and far between," said Queen Hippolyta. "I knew him as Stelios, but he was not always called by that name. As he gained in notoriety, it came to pass that he went by several names before settling on Stelios. Teris, I believe at one point was his name. And others claimed he was known as Zotikoz. An interesting choice of a name, as it means 'brimming with life.' And he was. Ha! Yes, he certainly was. Still, by the time he ventured beyond the walls of our city, he called himself Stelios."

"Stelios," Maia repeated. After a moment, she cocked her head. "It's a good name."

"You approve, do you? Well, yes, it is a good name as far as names go. Did you know him by another?" Queen Hippolyta asked.

"I didn't know him at all. But back home, his name was Matthias. Or Matt."

"And he named you Maia," said Queen Hippolyta. "Another interesting choice."

"My mother said he called me his 'little star' when I was born."

"Yes, well, he must have believed you would live up to such a name. It takes much courage to name a child after a goddess, even one whose light had been extinguished," offered Queen Hippolyta. "By your puzzled look, I presume you know little of your namesake. Maia was the eldest of the Pleiades and one of the more tragic examples of the chaos spawned by the war between the Olympians and the Titans. She did her best not to be embroiled in any of their ruinous affairs, so perhaps it was best she ended up with her sisters placed among the stars. But when Apollo, god of the sun, went dark, he took many stars with him, including the seven sisters. You joked of Orion's belt – his light dimmed as well. And many more would have been lost had Lord Zeus not made his bold gambit."

"Zeus told me his wife, Hera, also died," Maia said. "He told me right before he gave me the bracelet. I think he was trying to make me feel better about my father."

"Maia, my dear, it is almost sweet that you would think Lord Zeus to be concerned about your feelings, but sadly it is a foolhardy notion. The king of the gods was above all a cruel, selfish being that cared exclusively about his next meal and sexual conquest," said Queen Hippolyta, her face looking as though she'd caught a whiff of rotten fruit in the breeze. "Whatever he may have said to you, Hera did not die in the manner as did Apollo and some others. Lord Zeus robbing his wife of her godhood was tantamount to killing her, but she lived as a mortal for some time after the migration. She may be dead now, for all I know. I saw her but once after her fall – or push – from Mount Olympus before she went into hiding."

"If she was turned into a mortal, then she'd have to be dead," said Maia. "The migration happened a very long time ago."

"As I said before, there is a difference to how time passes in Olympia. And even the dead have a sneaky way of returning. Still, unlike Poseidon, she has not been seen in a very long time. The brother of Lord Zeus still manages to interfere every once in a while. It was from Poseidon that I learned of your existence."

"Poseidon is the god of the sea, right?" asked Maia.

"He *was* god of the sea. His son Triton took over for him after he stepped down. In fact, Triton may very well have survived the war between the gods," pondered Queen Hippolyta. "Unlike some of the other realms, the seas remain relatively safe."

"I met Triton. Well, I mean, I saw him the last time I was here. And he was back home too! He was watching me. I never got a straight answer about that. Why would the god of the sea leave Olympia to follow me?"

"He was no doubt following an order from Lord Zeus."

"No, I don't think so. Zeus didn't want anything to do with me. He was furious with King Alphaios for bringing me here," said Maia.

"Perhaps, but if forces were at play to bring you here, it would take someone of the greatest authority – and power – to send Triton to your world. If not Lord Zeus, then—"

"Poseidon! He could have sent him. You said that he still interferes."

"Interfere, yes, in the affairs of the people of Olympia, but it is unlikely that he holds enough sway in his mortal form to direct his son. Dorian the mortal is a far cry from Poseidon the god," said Queen Hippolyta.

"What did you call him?"

"After the migration, Poseidon assumed the name Dorian from the tribe that gave him refuge. Why does the name matter?"

"Because I have an uncle named Dorian," replied Maia. "He's my father's brother."

"Your father had no siblings."

"No, you're wrong. He has brothers back home – a lot of them. Most of them are jerks, but Dorian was okay, even with all the lies he told."

"I knew your father well, Maia. What you say is not possible."

"Dorian knew about Olympia. He even met me here after I escaped from King Alphaios. And he said my grandmother once knew about all of this too. They were his family. They must've all been from Olympia."

"Again, Maia, I do not profess to have any knowledge of your father that suggests he had a family," said Queen Hippolyta. "And he journeyed to your world alone."

Maia began pacing. "None of this makes sense. Could my Uncle Dorian be the same Dorian you're talking about?"

"Thou meant to ask, could your uncle be Poseidon?"

"I spoke to him not too long before coming back to Greece. He warned me not to come, and then I never heard from him again. I told him a Greek soldier had showed up in my house, and he said he would find out what the hell was going on over here," Maia said.

"A Greek soldier? You mean a soldier from Olympia?" asked Queen Hippolyta.

"I guess he was a soldier. His clothes were covered with blood," Maia recalled, glancing down at her own blemished tunic. "He had a warning – he said the son of Zeus was waiting for me."

"Lord Zeus had many sons, but none of any consequence since the fall of Mount Olympus with the exception of Heracles. In the past, his games were bothersome at best, but this is different altogether. That he would send someone for you is even more troubling than his attack on the Amazons," said Queen Hippolyta.

"So, you're okay with him trying to kill you?"

"You mistook my words. I expected him to come after me given our 'history.' After killing his mortal family in a fit of madness, Heracles was charged with completing twelve labours as a form of penance. My subjugation was amongst the tasks. It seemed inevitable that Heracles would oppose me again. Actions have a way of repeating themselves in Olympia."

"Zeus said the same thing to me," said Maia.

"*Hmmm.* Yes, well, Lord Zeus would know having created this place from the energies Hera and Poseidon gave forth. He would not allow for progress. It affects the memory of most – experiences or knowledge previously attained become cloudy at best. Those of us with greater knowledge of this world's creation have a sense, but the common denizens are truly surprised when history repeats itself."

"I think I know what you mean."

"Do you? Tell me, Maia. Have you ever held a sword?" asked Queen Hippolyta.

"Not a real one. After the soldier showed up in my house, I practiced using my lacrosse stick. But that was, well, that was just silly, I guess," Maia answered, somewhat embarrassed.

"You tried to prepare yourself against Heracles. I see nothing silly in that. Still, I imagine some formal training is warranted if the daughter of Stelios is to take a stand with the Amazons against Heracles. You look surprised, child. Is that not what you wanted?"

"Yes, it is, but... " Maia tried to finish her thought, but she found herself deprived of excuses. *But what?* The queen was offering protection – more than Uncle Dorian was able to. And more protection than her mother could ever ask for if she knew the quagmire into which Maia had stumbled. "But nothing. Yes. Please teach me to fight."

"We will do more than that. We will teach you to prevail," said Queen Hippolyta. "Let us find Captain Penelopeia. We start at once."

"Can we start tomorrow? I really should get home."

"And how may I ask are you going to do that? Lord Zeus's bracelet is less than reliable."

"Do you have a way of—"

"Breaching the barrier between our worlds? No, child, I do not. Alchemy was never my forte. Even if my sisters and I had time to study the elements, I doubt we would be able to replicate the work of Daedalus," said Queen Hippolyta. "Alas, even if I could help you return to your home, I would not. Your training must begin now."

"Queen Hippolyta, I am... so honored that you would train me. I just need to take care of some things back home so that my mother doesn't get the news that I've vanished," Maia said.

Queen Hippolyta rose and motioned to Bremusa, who waited several yards away on an embankment. "Maia, even if the bracelet does allow you to depart Olympia, there is no guarantee you will be able to return. If you leave now, you risk running afoul of Heracles. Ah, Bremusa, tell Captain Penelopeia to join me at the armory."

"Yes, my queen," Bremusa said before running back to the campsite.

"Maia, I will not force you to stay. If you need to tend to matters back home, you should go," said Queen Hippolyta. "I pray those gods that remain grant you safe passage."

"Thank you, your highness. I will come back," Maia vowed.

Queen Hippolyta placed her hand on Maia's shoulder. "And the Amazons will welcome you with open arms. Now, you would do best to exit our campsite's protective shroud before you attempt to use the bracelet again."

"A shroud? That's why I couldn't see the campsite until—"

"Until granted entry from this side. The Amazons are still afforded some protections from Gaia. Walk towards that fig tree. Once you pass it, you will clear the shroud. Good luck, Maia," said Queen Hippolyta.

"I'll take whatever luck I can get," Maia said softly. The fig tree grew some twenty yards away, but it may have well as been at the other end of a lacrosse field. Maia's legs fought her every step. She shuffled her feet several yards before Maia's mind agreed with her body. Leaving was a mistake, even if it was a chance to avoid panicking her mother. "Forgive me, Mom," Maia whispered, looking up at the clouds. They remained shapeless but were in some way a comforting reminder of her mother's own pluck. Maia turned around, but Queen Hippolyta had gone – to the armory to meet Captain Penelopeia, she presumed. Maia reached down and picked up a thick branch, carving a star in the dirt. After looking at it for some time, Maia crossed it out and threw down the branch.

"Does that mean you have come to a decision?" asked a man from the direction of the fig tree.

"You answer my question first," Maia replied. Turning around, she asked, "Should I call you Dorian or Poseidon?"

CHAPTER 15

GOD OF THE SEA

"YOU MAY CALL ME whatever you wish," answered Uncle Dorian.

"Are you sure you want to open yourself up like that? There's a lot of things I want to call you right now!"

"And you would be wholly justified in doing so. I lied to you."

"Lied to me? You *lied* to me? That doesn't even begin to cover your offenses," Maia yelled. "What are you doing here? Where've you been?"

"I was... detained. But I am here now, and I will help you return home."

"I don't want your help," Maia said. "Queen Hippolyta is going to train me."

"I do not think that is wise," said Uncle Dorian. "There is much more at play than even the queen of the Amazons knows. It is better that you leave."

"Were you spying on us? That's gross! How did you get past the shroud?" Maia asked.

"I have been afforded some privileges, Maia. These same privileges will allow me to return you to your home," said Uncle Dorian.

"Are you really Poseidon?"

"Maia, I can—"

"Yes or no!"

Uncle Dorian squinted as if blinded by the sun, though the clouds continued to cast shade upon the ground. Opening his eyes wide, he ran his hand along his chin, massaging an imaginary beard. Uncle Dorian pressed his lips until they were colorless before letting out an exaggerated breath. "I was god of the sea," Uncle Dorian answered, "until Lord Zeus asked me to relinquish my divinity as punishment for my part in the vast destruction caused by the Trojan War."

"And so my father—"

"Was not truly my brother," interrupted Uncle Dorian. "Maia, there is still much you do not understand. Please allow me to take you home. I will answer any of your questions once you have safely left Olympia."

Maia dropped to her knees, a sudden pain in her abdomen causing her to momentarily black out. Maia clutched her side, moaning in agony as hundreds of small knives stabbed her again and again.

"Maia!" Uncle Dorian called as he rushed to her side. "What is wrong?"

The pain isn't real, Maia told herself repeatedly. It's imaginary.

"Maia, are you hurt? What has happened to cause you such agony?"

"Shut up," Maia managed to say between breaths.

"Maia, I do not—"

Maia let go of her side and swung her fist, striking Uncle Dorian across his chest. "I said, shut up!" Uncle Dorian flew back several feet, a cloud of dust rising from where he hit the ground. What'd she done? Maia called his name, but Uncle Dorian didn't move.

Another stabbing pain caused Maia to grip her side. Maia winced as she heard the rustling of gravel. She looked at Uncle

Dorian – he remained still. The sound was coming from behind her. The person crept around Maia and stopped a few feet away. Maia raised her head and was met with a kick of dirt. Sputtering, Maia grimaced as a familiar and unwelcome face became clear.

"Impressive," said Akantha. "It is not everyday that you see a god knocked off his feet."

"Back away or you're next!"

"I doubt that very much. No, I intend to keep my promise, Maia. I am going to avenge my father," Akantha said, drawing her sword. "Titan's daughter or not, I will kill you."

Maia cocked her head. "What did you call me?"

"How pathetic. You still do not know who your father was? Then you are destined to die without that knowledge."

Akantha raised her sword. Maia stood, the pain in her side abating, but the anger she'd directed at her uncle remained. She turned around and grabbed a branch.

"You're going to fight me with a piece of wood?" Akantha taunted.

"A plank was good enough last time," Maia said. "Or did you forget landing on your face?"

"Oh, I remember, Maia. I remember everything."

"Then the pain I'm about to cause you is going to feel very familiar," Maia said, swinging the branch.

Akantha yelled as she charged, raising her sword over her head with both hands. Maia felt Akantha's sword slice through the air as she dodged the blow. Akantha stumbled past Maia, losing control of her momentum. Taking advantage of Akantha's overzealousness, Maia turned and grazed Akantha across the back with the branch. Akantha regained her footing and spun around, her sword missing Maia's throat by inches. Surprised, Maia threw her head back out of the way, but recovered after a moment. Fueled by rage,

Maia made eye contact with Akantha as she hurled the branch at her. Struck in the side of the head, Akantha cried out as she fell. Maia rushed over and leapt on top of Akantha, pinning her hands to the ground.

"It's over! Don't make me hurt you," Maia spat.

Akantha drew her knees up and knocked Maia off balance. Her right hand freed, Akantha punched Maia in the jaw before Maia returned the blow. Akantha grabbed Maia by the hair and yanked her to the side. Continuing to trade punches, Maia and Akantha rolled on the ground, dirt flying in every direction. With a well-placed elbow to Maia's ear, Akantha climbed on top of her. Maia put her fists together and punched Akantha in the shoulder, knocking her onto her back. Akantha rolled over and grabbed her sword, but Maia kicked it out of Akantha's hands before diving on top of her. Pinned once again to the ground, Akantha growled as she fought to break free.

"Ugh! Your vile sweat is dripping on me!"

"Not so tough without your sword, princess" said Maia. "What would your father think of you now?"

"Do not dare speak of my father!"

"And why not? You and everyone else don't have a problem talking about mine," Maia said, squeezing Akantha's wrists tighter.

"You are a fool if you think that this is how it ends," Akantha swore. Her eyes widened and teeth clenched in response to something or someone over Maia's shoulder. "Release me now, Maia, and I will have mercy."

Footsteps grew louder and faster, and Maia soon felt a gloved hand press into her shoulder. Maia didn't have to look to know that the hand belonged to Captain Penelopeia.

"Let go of her, Maia," said the captain.

"She tried to kill me! Like three times already," Maia said, jerking her shoulder to push off Captain Penelopeia's hand.

"Let go, Maia. Now!"

Gritting her teeth, Maia allowed Akantha some movement before one final shake and slam to the ground. Pushing herself off, Maia stopped next to Captain Penelopeia, who was flanked by Bremusa. Akantha jumped up with a shrill scream and lunged at Maia, but Captain Penelopeia blocked her with her sword and pushed her once more to the ground.

"Please, Akantha!" Bremusa cries. "You will make it worse."

Captain Penelopeia reached down and ripped off the sleeve of Akantha's tunic and used the material to bind Akantha's hands behind her. "You will go before the queen for judgment," Captain Penelopeia said, pulling Akantha to her feet. "You should have heeded my warning. It was wasted on you, clearly. Bremusa, take her."

"And what of her?" cried Akantha, trying to knock into Maia.

"Stop this, Akantha. She is not your concern. Pray that the queen is merciful. I would not be."

Bremusa stuck Akantha in the back with her spear, pushing her towards the campsite. "Watch where you put that!" Akantha complained. "*Ow!* Enough already. I will not resist."

When Bremusa and Akantha were out of sight, Captain Penelopeia asked, "Are you hurt?"

"I'm fine. Leave me alone. Don't you have more important matters to attend to?"

"The queen told me you had decided to leave."

"Well, yeah, about that... I, uh, changed my mind," said Maia.

"*Hmmm.* The queen suspected as much. She said I would find you lurking by the fig tree."

"Captain, I need to—"

"Who is that?" Captain Penelopeia interrupted, raising her hand to silence Maia.

"That's my uncle."

The captain continued to stare at Uncle Dorian's limp body, taking steps toward him. A few feet away, she jolted back. "Maia, that is the god of the sea."

"Yeah, he was the god of the sea at one point it turns out."

"Do not be so brazen. Did you do that to him?" Captain Penelopeia asked.

"I didn't mean to knock him out, but I was so furious at him," Maia answered, clenching her fists. "Do you think I hurt him?"

Captain Penelopeia kneeled beside Uncle Dorian, checking his pulse. "Deposed or not, he is a god of Olympus. He will recover."

"I think I should go talk to the queen."

"When she is finished dealing with Akantha, you may have an audience with her. Here, help me carry your 'uncle' back to the campsite," Captain Penelopeia said, lifting Uncle Dorian by the shoulders. "Though you are likely strong enough to carry him yourself by now."

"I am getting stronger," Maia said, grabbing Uncle Dorian's ankles. "It feels like he weighs less than a baby. To be honest, I'm trying not to freak out about it. What's happening to me?"

"You are achieving your potential."

"Just once, I'd like to get an answer from someone that doesn't raise more questions," Maia said, nearly dropping Uncle Dorian.

"For a flower to grow, Maia, a seed must be in the right place at the right time. The stars are in alignment for you to have the strength to fulfill your father's promise to Queen Hippolyta."

"My father promised something? Queen Hippolyta didn't say anything. What did he promise her?" Maia asked.

Captain Penelopeia stopped, a roguish grin on her otherwise stone face. "To kill the son of Zeus, of course."

CHAPTER 16

ONE LESS FOE

MAIA STARED AT CAPTAIN PENELOPEIA until she thought she would be able to adequately describe her features to a police sketch artist. The captain's unexpected smile vanished as quickly as it'd come, leaving her emerald green eyes and strong wide nose her most prominent features. Maia waited for Captain Penelopeia to explain herself, but with each passing second such an explanation seemed less and less likely to come.

"That's not funny," Maia said, pulling at Uncle Dorian's ankles.

"Nor was it meant to be, Maia," said Captain Penelopeia, readjusting her hold under Uncle Dorian's shoulder blades. "Your father vowed to protect the Amazons from Heracles. They had an interesting 'history,' your father and Heracles."

Maia and Captain Penelopeia hiked up an embankment, no words exchanged between them for several moments. Despite her uncle's size, it didn't cost Maia much to carry him.

"I have burdened you," said Captain Penelopeia as they cleared the ridge.

"I told you, he doesn't feel that heavy."

"Not with the god of the sea, but with the news of your father's promise."

"Oh, please, don't even start. Nothing surprises me," Maia retorted. "If I've learned to expect anything during my time in Olympia, it's that someone will eventually drop a bombshell on me about my father. I called this guy we're lugging my 'uncle,' but he admitted that he wasn't just before I smacked him. You say my father promised to kill Heracles, and I say, 'yeah, and what's next?' He and the queen had a hot and heavy romance?"

"Do not think my candor extends to an acceptance for such remarks about Queen Hippolyta. I would not hesitate to take— Bremusa!"

Captain Penelopeia dropped Uncle Dorian and swept past Maia. Following her path, Maia caught up as the captain skidded to the ground next to Bremusa, the side of her head soaked with blood. Captain Penelopeia put her arm under Bremusa's neck and cradled her.

"Open your eyes, my sister. This is not your time," said Captain Penelopeia, her words pulling Maia back to her first encounter with the Amazons.

Bremusa gently groaned and drew in a startled breath. Casting her wide eyes all around her, Bremusa cried out, "It was Marpe! She came upon us on horseback. We quarreled about the queen, and the last I remember is that she raised her shield." Bremusa put her hand to the side of her head, wincing from the touch. "Marpe must have struck me with it and taken off with Akantha."

"Easy, dear sister. We will get you help," said Captain Penelopeia, stroking Bremusa's uninjured temple. "Maia, stay here with Bremusa. Do not leave her."

"I won't. But what if Akantha and Marpe come back?" Maia asked.

"You have my permission to treat them as you did your uncle," Captain Penelopeia called as she ran towards the campsite.

"Not the answer I was expecting, I've got to say," Maia mumbled as she rushed over to Bremusa. "Can I do anything for you?"

"No, thank you. That man is your uncle?" said Bremusa.

"Yes," answered Maia. "Or no. It's complicated."

"Ha! You speak funny."

"Really? I wish it was funny," Maia said, kneeling sideways next to Bremusa. "What's Marpe's problem, by the way? I can't imagine anyone wanting to ride off with Akantha."

"She blames Captain Penelopeia, and by extension the queen, for the death of Skylla, a noble Amazon lost in battle against the forces of the son of Zeus. She and Marpe were close."

"Close enough to betray Captain Penelopeia?" Maia asked.

"Close enough, yes, to take arms against a fellow Amazon. I do pray that she comes to her senses before she brings further pain upon our sisters and the queen."

Maia heard a burst of footsteps. Captain Penelopeia returned with three other Amazons.

"Bremusa, is she—"

"I am well enough, my captain. Please allow Thais and the others to tend to me. You have far more urgent matters," said Bremusa, managing a tiny smile in spite of her obvious discomfort.

"Selfless Bremusa, I leave you in good hands," promised Captain Penelopeia. "Maia, help me lift... your uncle. The queen awaits our return."

"What are we going to do with him?"

"Nothing. We leave him in the care of the healers and wait for him to awaken," answered Captain Penelopeia.

"I can't believe he's still out."

"There can be no doubt or indecision on your part, Maia. You must learn to fight and channel your strength before another is hurt," Captain Penelopeia said, "or killed."

Maia shuddered. "Do you think he's going to be okay?"

"Thais will do her best to revive him."

"Maybe when he wakes up, he can somehow help me get word to my mother," said Maia. "He's able to breach the barrier between worlds."

Captain Penelopeia and Maia carried Uncle Dorian to a nearby tent. Grunting, Captain Penelopeia pushed open the flap of the tent and backed her way in. Maia ducked as she entered the tent. No sooner did the flap of the tent fall behind her, Maia's eyes began to burn.

"Ugh! What is that?" Maia asked, blinking her eyes and rubbing her nose against her upper arm.

"Herbs... potions... any variety of remedies that may help your uncle. Enough of your theatrics, Maia – we must see the queen!" commanded Captain Penelopeia.

"Where is she?" Maia asked as she stepped out of the tent behind Captain Penelopeia. "And what do you think is going to happen to Akantha?"

"I care not what outcome the fates have prescribed for the dishonorable princess. She has been given every chance to right herself, yet she has chosen to discard all she has been taught as an Amazon in the name of mere vengeance. Akantha is lost in every sense of the word. I will not speak for the queen, but I doubt she will allow Akantha to keep her sword and shield," Captain Penelopeia stated so plainly that Maia took her words as true, leaving her one less enemy about whom to worry.

Maia ran to keep up with Captain Penelopeia as they approached a tent almost as large as the queen's. The flap of the tent opened, and Queen Hippolyta stepped outside, followed by her guard "Bulldog."

"Ah, Captain Penelopeia, I see you have found our guest. It is good to see—what is the matter, captain?"

"Forgive me, your highness, but two of our sisters have brought shame upon us. Akantha has fled before she could be brought to you for again threatening Maia, and she did so with the assistance of Marpe," Captain Penelopeia recounted.

"Marpe? What would lead her to commit such an act? Unless... tell me, captain, was Skylla amongst those lost in battle while I was disabled?"

"Yes, my queen. She died protecting me, the guilt of which pains me greatly," said Captain Penelopeia.

"Nonsense! Skylla died with honor. Marpe is the guilty party. Skylla would certainly rebuke her lover for any treachery committed in her name," Queen Hippolyta said, placing a hand on Captain Penelopeia's shoulder. "Skylla was a courageous Amazon. She will not be forgotten. And every victory brought about through your leadership will further honor her memory."

"Thank you, my queen," Captain Penelopeia said, her head lowered. "Your benevolence is the utmost inspiration."

Maia felt a pressure building in her throat, making it difficult to swallow. Despite having witnessed truly dizzying acts of both horrible violence and gallant heroism during her visits to Olympia, observing this moment between the queen and the captain caused a swelling of emotion that Maia found impossible to suppress. Bringing her hand to her mouth, Maia bowed her head as tears streamed down her face. Gasping for breath, Maia fell to her knees.

"Child! What has happened?" Queen Hippolyta asked as she and Captain Penelopeia lifted Maia to her feet. "What causes you such sorrow?"

Maia continued to weep, her tears leading her to cough and sputter. The queen pulled her in close, and Maia rested her head on her shoulder. "I'm sorry," Maia managed to whisper between gasps of air.

"Do not apologize, child. You have endured much. There is no cause for embarrassment," said Queen Hippolyta, stroking Maia's hair.

"I'm not embarrassed, I'm just... so confused. Every time I think I know what I'm doing or feel like I've made the right decision, I get all mixed up again."

"And what decision have you made that brings you such bewilderment?" asked Queen Hippolyta. "You do not need to stay, child. If you worry about your mother, then you should—"

"Forgive me, my queen, but Maia does need to stay," interrupted Captain Penelopeia.

Queen Hippolyta and Maia looked at the captain in unison. Maia wiped her eyes and took a step away from the queen as she straightened herself up and turned completely to face Captain Penelopeia.

"What more do you need to tell me, captain?" asked the queen.

"I hit my uncle," Maia muttered, bowing her head again.

"More than hit, I dare say," said Captain Penelopeia. "Dorian, formerly of Mount Olympus, lies comatose in the tent of the healers, my queen. The child cannot control her strength. She must stay and be trained."

"For her sake or for ours, captain?" Queen Hippolyta asked.

"Your highness?"

"Forgive me, captain, but I detect more to your contention than mere concern for the safety of others on the receiving end of Maia's fist. You are proposing to make her an Amazon," said Queen Hippolyta.

"We could use her strength when we face Heracles," said Captain Penelopeia. "Moreover, it is what her father would have wanted."

Queen Hippolyta shook her head. "We cannot know that."

"He made a promise to—"

"Please, captain, do not speak in such a manner. He made many promises – he could not help himself! Stelios would have done anything for anyone. When he swore to aid us in vanquishing Heracles, I did not keep him to it. And there is no reason why Maia should be held accountable either. If she is to be trained, then it is her decision to make, free of any sense of obligation or need for recompense."

"Then we let her decide," said Captain Penelopeia, fixing her eyes upon Maia.

Maia stared back before shifting her eyes to the ground. A shadow fell between Queen Hippolyta and Captain Penelopeia made by the former's staff. Looking up, Maia noticed for the first time the adornment at the top of the queen's staff. It was a claw, perhaps that of an eagle, holding a small sphere. It reminded Maia of leading her lacrosse team to the championship. But it also reminded her of using her lacrosse stick to practice sword fighting, the memory of which made her blush.

"Maia, do you need time to make your decision?" asked the queen.

"No, your highness. I'm ready," Maia answered.

"Yes, I would say you are," said Queen Hippolyta.

"And I would say that you will be ready when I am done with you – ready to take on the son of Zeus," added Captain Penelopeia.

Maia nodded her head over and over. "Yeah, and anyone else who thinks I can't knock a god on his ass."

CHAPTER 17

THE SHROUD FALLS

FOR THE TENTH TIME in as many minutes, Maia was knocked to the ground. Groaning, she rubbed her left elbow, which took on a plum hue from having been landed on repeatedly.

"That was better."

"Um, what were you watching? I was belly up even quicker that time," Maia said.

"Do not speak that way to the queen!" commanded Captain Penelopeia.

"It is fine," said Queen Hippolyta. "What I meant is that you carried the sword with more assurance. Your fear was less evident. And though ultimately felled, your perception of your opponent was much improved."

"So, I looked good before I kissed the dirt again?"

"Yes," answered Queen Hippolyta. "On your feet."

"I think I need a break."

"We have barely begun, child. By the gods, I dare say she is more difficult than was Akantha," spat Captain Penelopeia. "My queen, may I be allowed to return to our troops?"

"Of course," said Queen Hippolyta.

Bowing to the queen, Captain Penelopeia cast her eyes upon Maia. The captain rose and hung her sword on her belt. She strode to where Maia's sword rested on the ground, picked it up, and speared it between Maia's feet.

"Hey! What the hell?"

"When receiving a blow from your opponent, set it aside with your flat and not the edge. And do not hesitate to counter. Sword fighting is not dancing. Be aggressive. Initiate – do not wait for your opponent to strike."

Maia put her hands on the pummel of her sword and heaved herself to her feet. Pulling the sword out of the dirt, Maia hung it on her belt before brushing the soil from her tunic. "Thank you for your advice, captain. But I don't think that I'm—"

Captain Penelopeia's sword cut through the air before Maia could finish making her excuses. Ducking to the side, Maia rolled on the ground and grabbed her sword in time to block the captain's next blow – *CLANG!* – using the flat as instructed. Captain Penelopeia leaned in, forcing their swords to meet at the guards. A buzzing filled Maia's ears from the noise made by the clash of the swords, but it was soon surpassed by Captain Penelopeia's breathing, increasing in raspiness until she sounded more like a gryphon than a person. Locking eyes with the captain, Maia dug her sandal-bearing feet into the ground and, gripping the sword until her knuckles were the color of her bruised elbow, pushed back. Her arms shaking, small gasps of breath and spit came in rapid succession from Maia's mouth. Clenching her teeth as a guttural noise swelled in her throat, Maia pushed her hands up-ward, a flicker of surprise registering in Captain Penelopeia's eyes.

"*GRRRRRRAAAAAAHHHHH!*" Maia yelled as she pushed the captain's sword aside. Reeling back, Maia swung her sword with both hands and batted Captain Penelopeia across her breastplate.

CLANG!

The captain teetered for a second, then with a groan dropped to her knees and fell forward onto her face.

"No! Oh no... oh no, Penelopeia... captain, what have I done?" said Maia, diving to her knees next to Captain Penelopeia. "Queen Hippolyta! I didn't mean to—"

"It is fine, child. I believe you have merely – and 'merely' is saying quite a lot when it comes to the captain – winded her."

"But is she going to be okay?"

"*Aaaaaarrrrr!*" Captain Penelopeia groaned. "What... what happened? How did—"

"I'm sorry! I was pushing back, but I didn't mean to hurt you. I just—"

"I told you not to apologize!"

"Sorry! No, I didn't mean that. I mean, I'm ju-ju-just so glad you're okay."

"Stop sputtering already and let me get to my feet."

"Captain Penelopeia, I would say that you taught Maia well today," said Queen Hippolyta.

"*Humph.* Too well, perhaps," agreed Captain Penelopeia.

"*Hmmm. Hmmm-huh. Ha ha ha ha haaah,*" laughed the queen.

"*Ha hah – kaff! kaff! – ha ha hah!*" joined the captain.

"I don't get it. Why are you laughing?" Maia asked.

"*Hmmm.* Why? Because opportunities for laughter are far too rare in these times. You should be proud of yourself. I do not recall when last Captain Penelopeia was brought down in combat."

"My queen! You exaggerate! I was not—"

"Do not take offense, captain. But had the son of Zeus been able to best you as such, he would have thrust his sword through your heart without hesitation. It is our good fortune that Maia is on our side," Queen Hippolyta said. "Heracles has much to fear from you, my child. Your strength is a match for his."

"Are you sure I'm ready for that?"

"Are *you* sure?"

"No, but a promise is a promise," Maia said, reaching for her sword. "Can we keep practicing?"

The Amazons looked at each other. Captain Penelopeia nodded slightly, and Queen Hippolyta smiled.

"Yes, child. But take caution not to hurt my captain."

"Your majesty!"

"I'll do my best," Maia said. "When do we get to use spears? And am I going to get a shield?"

"Wind me again, and I will gift you my shield," said Captain Penelopeia.

"Deal!" exclaimed Maia.

The captain let out a hearty laugh, but the crashing of thunder drowned it out. Streaks of lightning filled the sky, culminating in one explosive blast that electrified the air.

"My queen, the shroud!"

From above them, the sky rippled, waves of unseen energy spreading out in all directions before arching and striking the ground. The hairs on Maia's arms stood at attention as the temperature in the campsite immediately cooled. She looked to Queen Hippolyta for reassurance, but the monarch did little to hide her concern.

Queen Hippolyta threw down her staff and tore off her robe, revealing a suit of gold armor. Drawing her sword, she cried, "Quickly, captain, you must get the girl to safety!"

Stunned by the drastic turn of events, Maia stood as fixed as a statue until roused by Captain Penelopeia grabbing and pulling her by the arm. In the distance, Maia heard a terrifying scream. Turning in the direction of the noise, she witnessed a man in blackened armor bring down an axe, slicing an Amazon across her face.

"Captain, look!"

"Yes, I see, Maia," Captain Penelopeia cried. "Heracles's men have penetrated the campsite. You must head for cover."

"No, I want to help!"

"You are not ready, Maia. But fear not. We will make quick work of this. The son of Zeus has made a grave mistake." Captain Penelopeia pulled Maia through the campsite. All around them, men appeared as if from the ground itself. Captain Penelopeia fended off a number of attackers, never letting go of Maia. Not far ahead, a group of men circled Queen Hippolyta.

"To arms, sisters! To arms!" cried Queen Hippolyta as she cut down a pair of soldiers. "Where is your leader, fools? He dares not challenge the queen of the Amazons again." Queen Hippolyta swung around and stabbed one of Heracles's men through the chest. "If any of you survive long enough, you must tell Heracles that I welcome the opportunity to meet him in battle once more."

Captain Penelopeia pushed Maia to the ground, grabbing a spear from a fallen soldier. Several yards away, a man raised his bow and arrow with Queen Hippolyta in his sights. Captain Penelopeia leaned back and with a broad step thrust the spear through the air. The man pulled back on the bow, but before he released the arrow, he glanced in the direction of the path of the spear. He yelped as it impaled him in the eye.

"Maia, I must leave you. Go to the queen's tent and take cover until I come for you," barked Captain Penelopeia.

"But—"

"Go, Maia!" Captain Penelopeia shouted as she blocked an arrow with her shield. "You will fight another day."

Captain Penelopeia ran in the direction from which the arrow came, the bowman who sent it destined to meet with her sword. Maia sprinted to the queen's tent and dropped behind the flap covering the entrance, pulling it back just far enough to see the combat. All over the campsite, Amazons and Heracles's men exchanged blows from swords and spears. From her vantage point, Maia thought the Amazons were prevailing, but every so often she heard an Amazon cry out in pain, and she shut her eyes praying it was neither Queen Hippolyta nor Captain Penelopeia.

Peering from behind the flap, Maia sprang backwards as one of Heracles's men landed inches from her feet, his helmet rolling into the tent. The man just put his hands behind him to push himself off the ground when a sword skewered him through the chest. The queen's guard yanked back on the sword and spit on the fallen man before jumping back into the fighting. Maia crawled to the entrance. The man's head dropped to the side, and he looked at Maia. His eyes were wide and filled with panic. Maia strained not to look, but without a helmet to cover his face, Maia saw that he was likely no older than she. Within seconds, the look of fear in the man's eyes was gone, replaced by blankness. Maia retreated into the tent, her body trembling with revulsion at another encounter with death. She sat behind a pile of barrels and wrapped her arms around her legs. Outside of the tent, the sounds of the battle were unrelenting, and Maia put her hands to her ears and rested her forehead on her knees.

Behind Maia, the flap snapped open. Maia peeked out from the barrels. "Captain, is that—"

With a crash, the top barrel was knocked over by a shield held by Marpe – the Amazon who'd helped Akantha escape! "Get up," Marpe snarled.

Maia reached for a weapon, but Marpe kicked her arm. Pointing a sword at Maia's throat, Marpe said, "Do not be a fool. Heracles wants you alive, but I will not hesitate to give you scars to remember me by. Get up!"

The tip of the sword scratching against her chin, Maia did as she was told. Marpe continued to prod Maia with the sword, but Maia noticed Marpe's hands were not as steady as her tone of voice suggested. A loud crash outside of the tent caused Marpe to jerk around, and Maia took advantage of her distraction and ran, knocking a barrel over in her wake. Marpe kicked the barrel out of her path and blocked Maia from exiting the tent. Struck by Marpe's shield, Maia tumbled to the ground.

"I warned you," said Marpe, raising her sword. "Heracles will have to accept you scars and all."

"Why are you helping him? He wants to kill all of the Amazons!" Maia shouted.

"Queen Hippolyta and Captain Penelopeia have doomed our people. Heracles is merely carrying out what they have set in motion," said Marpe. "If I bring you to him, my fate is secure."

"He'll kill you too. Heracles is insane!" Maia countered.

Marpe's eyes shifted to the dead man's helmet resting on the ground. Keeping her sword pointed at Maia, Marpe bent down and picked up the helmet. "Put this on," Marpe commanded.

"No!"

"So be it," Marpe snarled before striking Maia in the side of the head with the helmet.

Maia slammed against the ground, a cascade of blurred stars dancing before her eyes until everything went hideously dark.

CHAPTER 18

MEETING THE ENEMY

MAIA VAULTED OVER THE STATUE of Zeus that lay broken in the middle of the lacrosse field. The king of the gods had been severed at his ankles, and Maia jumped again to clear his feet as soon as she hit the ground. Fragments of statues of the remaining gods of Olympus were scattered across the field like the ruins of an enormous chessboard. Dodging the head of Hephaestus, Maia extended her arms and caught a small star with her stick.

"Nice catch, firecracker!" called Nate from his seat on the remains of Aphrodite's left leg. "You're a shoo-in to get a medal tomorrow."

Maia twisted her stick again and again, trying to keep the star from melting the pocket. The smell of burning leather met her nostrils, and Maia gave up, hurling the star back to the heavens. It rose and settled in the middle of a constellation that looked like the head of Mickey Mouse.

"Man, that's a real shame," said Nate, sliding off Aphrodite. "I thought we'd keep at least one."

Maia jammed her stick in the ground. Immediately, it began to vibrate. All around her, the broken bits of the gods of Olympus began to shake, and soon the entire field was swaying. Maia fell back, hitting her head on Hephaestus's deformed hand.

"Dang! That was a big one! You reckon the gods don't like us playing on their graves?" Nate asked once the ground stopped quaking.

Maia rubbed the back of her head, sensing a 'goose egg,' as her grandfather would call bumps and bruises after she took a tumble on the playground.

"Hey, check it out! Here comes another one. I got it this time," called Nate, grabbing a lacrosse stick. Nate dashed across the field, all but tripping over the staff of Hermes in pursuit of the falling star. He'd just about grazed the star with the scoop of his stick when he disappeared over the edge of the field.

Maia ran to where Nate had taken his last steps and peered over the side. There was nothing to see but a swirling mass of stars and clouds. Nate was gone! Maia shifted into a cross-legged position and spun around. The lacrosse field had transformed into a classroom, and a familiar figure stood at the board holding a spear.

"Maia, can you come back to your seat now?" asked her school counselor, Mr. Foster.

Maia shifted her feet at the back of her chemistry classroom. All of the seats had been replaced with broken columns or tree stumps. Mr. Foster came around the teacher's desk in front of the board and tapped the spear repeatedly on the floor.

"I'm not letting you out of here until you've hit the bull's-eye at least once," Mr. Foster said, pointing to a target on a tree outside the classroom window.

Maia dragged her feet as she made her way up to the front of the classroom. The smell of horse manure wafted in from the open windows. Maia wrinkled her nose as she tried to figure out from which window the smell was coming, but there was nothing outside except for the tree painted with the target.

"Maia, you can do this!" said Mr. Foster, holding out the spear.

Maia took a hold of the spear, but Mr. Foster pulled it back as it transformed into a blood red, two-headed serpent. With a hiss, one of the heads reeled back and then dove in, biting Mr. Foster on his hand. He opened his mouth to scream, but the lone sound was the ringing of the bell hanging over the door of the classroom. The din grew and grew until the bell fell from the wall and crashed on the mismatched tiles below. The floor began shaking, and a crack formed between Maia and Mr. Foster. The shaking became more and more violent until Maia lost her footing and fell forward into the crack – and out of her dream, woken by the galloping of a horse. She was strewn across its back on her stomach.

Maia winced in pain from the blow she'd taken from Marpe, who she could now see was riding the horse. Maia was wearing the helmet with which Marpe had hit her. The shaking from her dream matched the furious pace of the horse. Maia cringed again as she turned her wrists, which were bound together with some coarse, sharp material.

Marpe took no notice of Maia being awake, or, if she did, Maia surmised, she didn't care or acknowledge it as they cleared a field peppered with fig and olive trees. The horse slowed, and Maia managed to turn her head. Several yards away, two men sat on horseback. As they drew closer, Maia recognized one of them as the man who'd surprised her in her living room weeks ago. He was wearing dull gray armor in contrast to the bright gold worn by his companion.

The horse skidded to a stop, and Maia closed her eyes, thinking it best to pretend to be unconscious. The horse whinnied and stomped its hooves, bringing up a cloud of dust.

"Easy, easy! *Whoa!*" ordered Marpe, providing cover for Maia as she was unable to not cough from all of the dust.

"I thought the Amazons were expert equestrians," said the man in golden armor.

"*Whoa!*" cried Marpe again, the horse settling in at last. "I am an Amazon no more. Where is Heracles? I have the girl."

"That does not look like a girl," said the man in gray.

"She wears a helmet, you fool. It is the helmet of one of your dead brothers," spat Marpe. "I had to sneak her out during the attack."

"Take it off!" the man in gold commanded.

Maia kept her eyes closed as Marpe wrenched the helmet off her head. "There, see! This is the girl your lord seeks," said Marpe.

"Yes, it is. I recognize her from... " began the man from Maia's living room.

"From where?" asked Marpe.

"Pay no mind. Bring her here!"

"*Heeya!*" barked Marpe, prodding her horse to draw closer to the men.

"On behalf of Lord Heracles, we thank you for your service," said the man in gray.

"And here is your reward," said the man in gold, followed by a whistling sound and a cry of pain from Marpe. Maia blinked her eyes open to witness Marpe tumbling off the horse, blood flowing from where her neck had once been attached to her head.

The man in gray grabbed Maia by the neck and pulled her closer to his horse. Maia lifted her head and bit the man's wrist, the taste of dirt and oil filling her mouth. With a curse, the man jerked his hand back, releasing his grip. Maia slid off the horse and dropped on top of Marpe's decapitated corpse. Rolling over, Maia leapt up and darted towards the trees.

"Get her!" cried the man in gray, rubbing his wrist.

The man in gold snorted with laughter. "And just how far do you think she will get, Alastor?"

Maia wondered that herself. She passed the first tree when she heard the clip-clopping of a horse, not from behind her but from the trees. Maia swerved and raced in another direction. Heracles's men whipped their horses into action. Maia caught herself on a large branch. As she pulled at her sleeve, a horse burst through the trees. Its rider grabbed her by the shoulder and knocked her to the ground. The horse scampered off as the rider jumped on top of Maia. Over the curses of Heracles's men, she looked into her Uncle Dorian's deep blue eyes as he crushed an object in his hand that emitted a familiar but undesired flash of blinding light.

CHAPTER 19

NO SUCH PROMISE

MAIA RUBBED FURIOUSLY at her eyes, futilely trying to regain her vision. "Ugh! What did you do that for?" she shouted as her uncle came into view.

"Whatever do you mean, Maia?" Uncle Dorian asked, straightening his clothes, which like Maia's were no longer in the mode of Olympia. "I did not intend to hurt you by jumping on top—"

"Not that! Why did you bring me home? We have to go back!" Maia screamed, skimming the ground with her hand. Though the ropes that bound her wrists were gone, the cuts they'd caused remained.

Uncle Dorian brushed the dirt off his pants. He reached out a hand and helped pull Maia to her feet. Drawing her in close, Uncle Dorian squinted his eyes and whispered, "Are you insane? We are not going back."

"Let go of me!" Maia yelled, pushing Uncle Dorian aside. She retreated a few steps. "How can you just walk away?"

"Walk away? I am not walking away from anything. I have fought long and hard for the continued existence of Olympia. But even I know when to give up. Olympia is on the verge of ruin. Heracles will rain fire upon his father's fabrication until there is nothing left. Despite your desire to put yourself in harm's way, I owe it to your mother and father to keep you safe."

"Well, you've done a lousy job of protecting me. Where've you been?" Maia asked.

"I had matters to attend to when I arrived in Olympia after our telephone conversation. Unfortunately, these matters swiftly became rather complicated," said Uncle Dorian, "and I found myself... detained."

"By Heracles?"

"No, Maia. It had nothing to do with Heracles or your current situation," answered Uncle Dorian.

"Then you should've forgotten about it," scolded Maia.

"Do not be so impudent, Maia. Not everything that occurs in Olympia has direct bearing on you. But that does not mean it is, or was, unimportant. Regardless of my other responsibilities, your safety was my priority – then and now – which is why you are not returning to Olympia."

"I'm not safe here either! Besides, I have to go back. My father made a promise to the Amazons, and I'm going to keep it," said Maia.

"I am not aware of any such promise," said Uncle Dorian, frowning. "What promise do you believe he made?"

"He promised to kill Heracles."

Uncle Dorian stared at Maia for several seconds, his brow furrowed. Then, shaking his head, he said, "No, Maia. Your father would have made no such promise."

"Yes, he did! Captain Penelopeia told me, and the queen, well, she confirmed it," Maia said, crossing her arms.

"Maia, your father may have had every reason to hold Heracles in contempt, but to promise to kill him?" said Uncle Dorian. "No, not your father."

"What is that supposed to mean, 'had every reason'? If my father and Heracles had some type of—"

"It does not matter," interrupted Uncle Dorian. "It is quite literally ancient history."

"Don't do that. Don't say something about my father and then – *pbbbt!* – nothing. What's the big deal anyway? He's dead! You don't have to be so secretive about him," cried Maia.

"Your father is not dead, Maia," said Uncle Dorian.

Maia felt the blood drain from her face, leaving her a ghostly white. "What did you say?" she asked though Uncle Dorian's words still rang in her ears.

"Your father is not dead in the 'classic' sense," answered Uncle Dorian. "I thought you understood."

"But everybody talked about his 'sacrifice.' Even you. I can't believe... he's not dead," said Maia, leaning forward and bracing her hands on her knees. While she took several deep breaths, the possibility of passing out still felt very real.

"Maia, please do not make yourself ill," said Uncle Dorian as he came to Maia's side and put his hands on her shoulders. Maia looked at him sideways and with a final prolonged inhalation jerked her shoulders as she straightened herself. Knocked aside, Uncle Dorian trod away from Maia and folded his arms, one hand rubbing his chin.

"Where is he?" Maia asked. "Where is he, Uncle Dorian? If he's not dead, then I want to know where he's been all of my life!"

"In Olympia, of course," Uncle Dorian stated. "His 'sacrifice,' not unlike mine, was for the preservation and betterment of Olympia. When he resisted coming back after meeting your mother and producing you, he sealed his own fate."

Maia rubbed her wrists where they'd been tied together. Holding out her arm, she counted three murky black bruises she'd acquired sparring with Captain Penelopeia. Maia made a fist, picturing herself holding a sword. Turning to Uncle Dorian, she said, "We're going back."

"Maia, that is—"

"We're going back," Maia cut in, "and then you're going to take me to my father."

"I will do no such thing," Uncle Dorian snapped.

"Yes, you will. You're going to bring me to my father, and then we're going to help the Amazons. That's the end of the story. And if you don't do what I'm asking, I'll blow the lid off this whole thing. I'll tell my mother everything."

"With all respect to your mother, your disclosure of the existence of Olympia would be of no consequence. There is nothing she could do," said Uncle Dorian.

"Uncle Dorian... Dorian... Poseidon... oh, whatever the hell you call yourself, if my father is alive or not dead in the 'classic sense,' then you owe it to me and my mother to bring me to him. You need to make things right," Maia pleaded. "You need to fix what your stupid Lord Zeus started all those centuries ago. Please, Uncle Dorian, I'm asking this of you after everything I've been through. Don't make me beg."

Uncle Dorian remained silent. A raindrop made an ant-size crater in the dirt at Maia's feet. Another hit Uncle Dorian on the side of his nose, but he didn't react. He tilted his head back as several more drops fell. Within seconds, the sky cracked open, and Maia and Uncle Dorian found themselves under siege from the rain. Maia's shirt changed from a light to dark blue, but still Uncle Dorian said nothing. After a flash of lightning cut through the sky, he lowered his head with an almost imperceptible smile. "Very well, Maia," Uncle Dorian said at long last, "but do not expect events to go as you hope."

"I never have," Maia countered, "not since the day Icarus shot an arrow at me."

"Being shot with an arrow should be the least of your worries."

INTERLUDE II

ONE DAY BEFORE THE CREATION OF OLYMPIA

HERA, WIFE OF ZEUS and queen of the gods, reached out her hand to stroke one of the hundred lifeless heads of Ladon, the massive serpentine dragon that guarded the garden of the Hesperides. The creature's pallid corpse was pocked with eyelet shaped wounds as if stabbed by thousands of miniscule daggers. Kneeling, Hera leaned forward and kissed the beast, resting the side of her head on it. Hera's chin quivered. Tears of shimmering silver pooled by her ear.

"Is this necessary?" asked Poseidon, god of the sea, as he spat onto the scorched ground, inches away from another of Ladon's heads.

"Do not soil my garden further!" Hera cried, wiping her eyes as she rose up from her position of mourning. "Ladon was a faithful servant."

"You demean yourself, sister. He was your dog," said Poseidon.

"Ladon was no more a dog than your son Polyphemus. And mourn him you did, brother, after he perished," countered Hera.

The ground beneath the Olympians shook. "You dare compare my son—"

"A Cyclops!"

"He was my son, Hera. This over-gorged snake," Poseidon said as he paused to kick another of Ladon's heads, "is not worth the genuflection of the queen of the gods."

"Enough!" thundered Lord Zeus, king of the gods. "You squabble like children while your master plots to save Olympus. Look around you. The dragon is far from the sole trace of death in your garden, Hera." Zeus's eyes burned as he surveyed the smoldering rinds and charred trunks surrounding them. "Let the rotting fruit of the orchard remind you of all that is at stake. The golden apples born from Gaia's fruited branches would no more provide sustenance to a satyr than grant immortality."

"Your cruelty has no limits, my husband. Why did you bring us here? What role could the father of the Hesperides play in your salvation? He has not spoken since his betrayal by your son Heracles. The Titan will not aid you," said Hera.

"My sightless wife, you underestimate Atlas. Though Lord Zeus himself condemned the son of Iapetus to shoulder the sky these many centuries, he will not remain silent. Now," Zeus began as lightning encircled his hands, "let us honor your pet." Zeus clasped his hands together. The foul air emanating from Ladon's corpse crackled as Zeus pulled his hands apart, releasing a ball of lightning that incinerated the dragon like so much kindling.

"Thank you, my lord," whispered Hera.

"Can we not proceed?" hissed Poseidon. Shaking, the sea god raised his fist in a fit of anger – but wanting for his powerful trident. He turned his fist over before grunting and opening his hand.

"Triton will honor your realm, brother," proclaimed Zeus.

"Do not condescend to me, 'mighty sky god.' I accept my punishment readily, but will no longer tolerate your petty tyrannies. You won. Since the Titanomachy you have sought my renouncement. Why settle for the sky when you can have domain over the seas? This war has afforded you the opportunity to seize control of all realms in the universe."

"You see this as a consolidation of power? You are foolish, brother. Had Lord Zeus sought control of the seas and the Underworld after our decade of battle with the Titans, it would have been so," said Zeus, arcs of lightning dancing between his fingertips. "Our brother Hades labors to contain the dead. The Underworld overflows with mortals and immortals alike. Lord Zeus no more seeks control of the Underworld than of the seas. Your son will hold your trident. That is law."

"We shall see, brother," countered Poseidon. The sea god pushed past Zeus and Hera, the remains of the trees in his path shaking from the roots up to their splintered branches. "Atlas awaits us at the ends of the earth."

"My lord, how can you be so certain Atlas will grant you what you seek?" Hera asked, pressing her body against Zeus.

"Because Lord Zeus will grant the Titan what he has long sought – his freedom," answered Zeus.

"My lord?"

"For Olympus to survive, Atlas must renounce his 'throne' as well," answered Zeus. Holding out his hand, he added, "Come, wife. Let us finish this. Lord Zeus, that is, *I* wish to torture you no longer."

Hera's fingers trembled as she took her husband's hand, her face reflecting both surprise and sadness at his gesture of kindness. Hand in hand, the king and queen of the gods strode through the garden of the Hesperides in Poseidon's wake, taking care not to step on the decaying fruit littered about. A heavy curtain of smoke and haze blocked their path. Hera squeezed Zeus's hand, and he in turn smiled at his wife. Unblinking, Zeus thrust his free hand skyward, clutching a bolt of lightning as it materialized. Slowly, Zeus opened his hand, and the discharge of lightning burned a clearing.

Hera gasped at the sight of a body a few steps away. It was a nymph.

"My lord, it is—"

"Aegle," Zeus finished. "The nymph's light has been extinguished. As Ladon perished, so did the daughters of Atlas, your faithful gardeners."

"This is too much, husband," said Hera, her eyes wet with tears. "Please end my suffering."

Zeus and Hera completed their procession in silence, coming to stand beside Poseidon at the fringe of the garden. Ahead of the gods lay a lifeless space void of light – the one sound heard was a rhythmic rasping not unlike that of an aged engine soon made to falter.

"He has thus far ignored my entreaties," said Poseidon.

"You have nothing to offer him, brother," countered Zeus, "whereas Lord Zeus holds the key to his cell." Zeus stepped forward and bended one knee to the ground. "Atlas, son of Iapetus, grant the king of the gods an audience."

"You too, brother? You humble yourself before one so unworthy as Atlas? He earned his punishment," cried Poseidon. "You are mad to—"

BOOM!

The bolt of lightning caught Poseidon in his chest, flinging him into the charred remains of the orchard.

"My lord!" cried Hera, running to Poseidon's side. "How can you be so cruel?"

Zeus held out his hand, his palm facing Hera. Poseidon moaned, and Hera, heeding her husband's warning, tended to the god of the sea rather than continuing her questioning.

"Atlas," Zeus continued, "do not stand in silence. Lord Zeus has come to make reparations." The rasping noise grew stronger and heavier. Zeus rose. "Your punishment is at an end."

Silence filled the void. Behind Zeus, Poseidon groaned as Hera pulled him to his feet. A light twinkled in the void, followed by another and another, until a shape took form. Balancing on the edge of the garden stood a massive figure made of swirling stars, moons, and fathomless stellar masses. On his shoulders rested an orb of infinite size, itself enclosing a palette of planets, nebulae, and constellations.

"DO... NOT... TAUNT ME, GODLING!" boomed a voice that tore through the garden, knocking Poseidon onto his back again. "LEAVE ME... TO MY BURDEN."

"Lord Zeus will not allow that, Atlas," said Zeus, his olive skin showing the faintest hint of crimson over his jutting cheekbones. "You have suffered from my arrogance and mistrust long enough." Arching his spine, Zeus drew his arms back, and when he thrust his arms forward, a surge of lightning seared Atlas's right knee.

"*AARRRGHHH!* WHAT ARE YOU DOING, GODLING?" roared Atlas. "YOU WILL DESTROY US ALL!"

Zeus reared back, his hands shaking above him as he clutched some unseen energies that soon formed a bubble of electricity. As the bubble expanded, Zeus struggled to contain it before finally launching it at Atlas, striking the Titan in his left shin.

"My lord, what madness is this?" cried Hera over Atlas's agonizing screams. "If Atlas lets the orb fall, the heavens will—"

"Have faith, my wife. Our world has gone mad, but Lord Zeus has not," called Zeus as he cast bolt after bolt of lightning at Atlas. The putrid air of the garden was burned clean by the radiant shocks of washed out gold generated by the attack. Zigzags of lightning ripped through the charcoal sky, embraced by Zeus and redirected towards Atlas.

Over the furious din of explosive cracks and thuds, Atlas could be heard to produce a rueful tone that seemed to herald his fall. Atlas's colossal frame was slashed like so much grass by a scythe. His moans grew in sickening strength until Zeus at last lowered his hands. And then, like the leaf of a tree in the last days of autumn, Atlas fell onto the charred soil of the garden. Above him, contrary to Hera's fears, the orb hung in place. As he lay groaning, the inky cloak of celestial bodies that had covered Atlas were leeched into the sky from his skin, revealing a pale olive complexion.

"What have you done?" asked Atlas, his voice drained of its deep tenor. "The heavens cannot sustain!"

"But were that so, Atlas. Then Lord Zeus would have far less guilt. The heavens will not fall. Nor would they ever have. It was my gamble to keep you and your strength contained while your brothers and sisters safely rotted in Tartarus," said Zeus. "You could have stepped down long ago. However, you kept your post, even after Heracles attempted to—"

"Do not mention that bastard! He was the one who—"

"Should have made you realize that you could choose freedom. Still, you did serve a purpose – a purpose that ultimately thwarted Lord Zeus's efforts. As long as you held the heavens in place, Lord Zeus could not make the alterations to space and time required to save our kind. Now, rise. Lord Zeus has much to—"

"Alter reality? Long may I have held the heavens in place, but I dare say you lack the power to enact such change," said Atlas. "What forces do you command to make such a claim?"

"Our godhood, Titan. My brother will rob Hera and me of our energies to create a new world," said Poseidon as he limped across the garden aided by Hera.

"Impossible!" cried Atlas. "Your wife and brother are weak, godling. They do not possess the power to fuel your efforts."

"And what do you know of this?" asked Zeus, his contempt failing to mask his concern at Atlas's allegation. "Lord Zeus does not make false promises."

"Take mine," said Atlas.

"What foolishness is this?"

"Take my power. It will allow you to complete your task. Though freed of my burden, I no longer wish to be immortal," said Atlas.

"Very well, Titan," responded Zeus. "For the glory of Olympus, Lord Zeus accepts your sacrifice."

"I care not for your glory. My sacrifice is made to protect the mortals that have suffered long enough under your reign," said Atlas. The Titan walked to the edge of the garden and peered over the side before facing Zeus. "Get on with it, godling."

CHAPTER 20

THE JAGGED PIECE

MAIA SHOVED THE LAST of her clothes into her suitcase. Her blue shirt was still wet from the deluge she'd been caught in with Uncle Dorian the day before, and Maia left it to dry in the bathroom. Maybe Jackie would pack it with her belongings when she left Krestena in the next couple of days. Maia zipped her suitcase shut and jerked it off her bed. She took a quick glance around the room. The book she'd read on the airplane, *The True Story of Greek Mythology*, was on Jackie's nightstand. Maia bit her bottom lip as she thought of how good a friend she had in Jackie. She stretched to ease the knot of pain digging into her side. Jackie said her goodbyes before Maia had gotten in the shower. She was headed to a café around the corner from the hotel for a planning meeting with some participants she'd become friendly with at the museum, including the formerly annoying Roc, who once again piqued Jackie's curiosity. Maia wasn't pleased with abandoning her friend, but Jackie understood and even encouraged her to go, though it meant Jackie would continue the ambassador program without her. Maia took some comfort in knowing Jackie wouldn't be without companionship.

Maia pulled her suitcase into the hallway. One of the wheels caught on a raised corner of the door saddle, causing Maia to lose her grip and the suitcase to tumble onto its side. So much for a

quiet exit, Maia thought. As she kneeled down to pick it up, someone else's hand beat her to it.

"So, this is for real, firecracker? You're quitting?" asked Nate,
his eyebrows raised to almost impossible heights above his green
eyes. He was squeezing the brim of his baseball cap with his other
hand so tightly that Maia imagined it'd never go back to its
intended form. "I didn't take you for a quitter."

"I'm not quitting, Nate. I'm going to see my grandmother for a
few days, and then I'll meet up with you in Athens. She's sick, and I
can't take the chance that I may never see her again," Maia lied. "I
know it sucks, but what am I supposed to do?"

"Well, you could start by telling the truth," Nate said, pulling
Maia's suitcase down the hallway.

"What the hell are you talking about?" Maia asked, her voice
cracking with her lame attempt to cover up her shock. "I'm not
lying. My uncle came all the way to Krestena to find me and bring
me to see my grandmother."

Nate continued down the hallway, through the common room,
and into the lobby before turning to face Maia. "Whatever you got
going on, just be careful. I expect to see you in Athens in one
piece."

"Nate, I don't—" Maia began, but Nate's kiss prevented her from
any further fabrication. Maia's cheeks burned. Pulling away, she
asked, "What was that for?"

"For luck, of course. Watch your back," Nate demanded as he
brushed past Maia, her face still a shade as red as a poppy. "And
here," Nate added, tossing Maia his baseball cap. "Hold onto that
until Athens."

"I'm not wearing an 'A's' cap," Maia said.

"I wasn't expecting you to wear it. It probably wouldn't fit
under a helmet," Nate said, disappearing into the common room.

Maia hardly had time for Nate's words to register before a car blasted its horn out on the street. Startled, Maia dropped Nate's cap. "Under a helmet," Maia repeated as she bent down to pick it up. "What the—"

BLLLAAATTT!

Maia peered through the window of the front door. Uncle Dorian was waving at her to come to the car he'd rented. Maia hurried onto the street. Uncle Dorian met her by the trunk and tossed her suitcase inside, revealing foul patches of sweat under his arms. Uncle Dorian's hair, always meticulously combed, looked suitable for occupancy by a family of birds.

"What took you so long?" he asked, his eyes as crazed as a court jester's.

"I was, uh, talking to someone. Could anyone else possibly know what's going on with me?"

"What do you mean? Your mother – though I am still amazed – spoke to the organizers of your program and gave consent for you to leave," said Uncle Dorian, his voice volume falling to a whisper. "They believe that I am taking you to Varkiza to see your grandmother."

"No, not that. I'm asking about Olympia. Something bizarre just happened," Maia said. "There's a boy who—"

"Get in the car," Uncle Dorian ordered, slamming the trunk closed.

Maia opened her mouth to protest, but Uncle Dorian was sitting behind the steering wheel before she could verbalize her annoyance. She yanked open the front passenger door and slid into the car. "I was telling you something important, jackass!"

Without a word, Uncle Dorian peeled away from the curb to the bleating of multiple car horns. Maia tugged at her seatbelt, managing to click the buckle in place before Uncle Dorian stopped short behind a fruit delivery truck. Uncle Dorian pounded his fist on the dashboard.

"Um, I realize we're about to go into battle, but try not to get me killed before we get there," Maia said, her eyes boring a hole in Uncle Dorian's right temple.

"A boy said what, Maia? A boy suggested that he knows about Olympia? Of course it is possible! Chaos is what awaits us there. I have no way of knowing who may have journeyed back and forth to Olympia. A soldier of Heracles attacked you in your house – in America! That should be impossible, but yet... so, yes, the boy could know." Craning his neck out the window, Uncle Dorian stomped on the gas pedal and swerved around the truck, again to a chorus of horns. "If you have no additional concerns, we can begin our suicide mission."

* * *

MAIA FOLLOWED UNCLE DORIAN as he raced through the woods. She was able to make out the occasional curse from the string of his ramblings, which was hardly the support she was seeking. Uncle Dorian stopped and rested his hand upon an oak tree, its branches twinned with a nearby poplar tree. "This is your last chance to stop this crusade," Uncle Dorian said through gritted teeth.

"I'm not going to change my mind, Uncle... What do you want me to call you?"

"Dorian will suffice. It is a name I have known long enough," answered Uncle Dorian. "When we journey to Olympia, we will be on the outskirts of the Amazons' campsite. I do not know what we will find, Maia. When I set off after you and that Amazon—"

"Her name was Marpe."

"When I set off after you and that treacherous wench, Marpe, the Amazons were still engaged in battle with Heracles's men. Queen Hippolyta seemed to be leading her warriors to victory, but there were fallen Amazons as well. We may find this all for naught."

"Even if the Amazons were defeated, you're still taking me to see my father. And if we have to go up against Heracles, then that's what has to be," Maia said, picking up a branch.

"With a stick? You will challenge the son of Zeus with kindling? Maia, if the Amazons are no more, then you must reconsider your plan."

"Well, there's just one way to find out," Maia countered. "Get your flash-bulb thing out."

Uncle Dorian shook his head as he reached into his pocket. He pulled out a brown fist-size bag that reminded Maia of the faux leather sack she kept marbles in as a girl. Uncle Dorian untied the bag's strings and pulled out a flat, quarter-size piece of stone. He stuffed the bag back in his pocket, holding the fragment in his fist. "Close your eyes."

"Wait! What the hell is that?" Maia asked, pointing at Uncle Dorian's clenched hand. "Where's the—"

"Flash-bulb? Yes, the remnants of Pandora's box emit a blinding light when crushed, but there is no 'bulb' of any sort," said Uncle Dorian, opening his fist to show Maia the jagged piece of pottery in the palm of his hand. "It may appear fragile, but the energies it holds are strong enough to pierce the boundaries between our worlds when released."

"That's a piece of Pandora's box?" asked Maia.

"Have you heard of my brother's cruel creation? Angered by the theft of fire, Zeus created Pandora, the gift bearer, to hold a jar – some idiots called it a box – containing all of the hardships and illnesses that could ultimately plague mankind. Though instructed not to open the jar, Pandora could not subdue her curiosity, and she released the evil spirits contained within, eternally robbing man of peace. It was Daedalus who discovered that the unique properties of the jar – once emptied even of Hope – could be used as a means of passage."

"Icarus shot me with an arrow," Maia said, rubbing her head. "He didn't use anything like that."

"The artificer's son was always one for showmanship," Uncle Dorian sneered. "The arrow contained a piece of the jar. Its energies were released when the arrow struck you. Your bracelet also holds fragments of Pandora's box."

"But wasn't Icarus taking an awfully big chance that the arrow would kill me?" Maia asked, her thoughts racing back to the beach in Varkiza and her initial desire to knock Icarus out.

"Far be it for me to defend that fool, but the arrow likely possessed no head. He sought to impress you, not cause your death. Now, if we are done with the history lesson—"

"How big was Pandora's box?" interrupted Maia. "There seems to be a lot of pieces of it floating around."

"It was *HUGE*, okay? It took a bloody huge jar to hold all the world's evils! Can we get on with this?" asked Uncle Dorian, waving his arms about like a damaged windmill.

"Alright, alright! Let's do it," Maia said, keeping her eyes fixed on the piece of Pandora's box, welcoming the release of energy while praying it would not be the last time she experienced its brilliance.

CHAPTER 21

A WARRIOR'S WEAPON

THE RANKNESS OF THE FUNERAL PYRE could be sensed far beyond the confines of the Amazons' campsite. Maia grabbed Uncle Dorian's hand as soon as they'd traversed the barrier between the two worlds. Too late, she thought. But then Uncle Dorian squeezed her hand and said, "Listen." Also springing from the direction of the campsite were cries of celebration. Maia and Uncle Dorian raced across a swampy meadow to the campsite, where they were equally pleased and dismayed to see the Amazons gathered around a massive bonfire chanting the names of their fallen sisters. In the middle of the crowd of warriors stood a solemn Queen Hippolyta with faithful Captain Penelopeia by her side.

Maia pushed her way through the mass of mourners. She got two feet away from the queen when a spear blocked her path. "Bulldog" grabbed Maia by the neck and lifted her to the tips of her toes. Maia managed a barely audible gurgle, but mercifully it was loud enough to gain the attention of Queen Hippolyta.

"Pantariste, release her!" commanded Queen Hippolyta. "I thank you for your steadfast loyalty, but there has been more than enough bloodshed in recent hours."

Maia fell to her knees. "*Huff huff huh!*" She put her hand to her neck and rubbed her throat. "Bulldog" (a.k.a. Pantariste) could easily scale the Empire State Building with her extraordinary grip. Between coughs, Maia managed, "I... take it – *kaff! kaff!* – you won?" Maia attempted to stand, but her legs failed her and she fell on her bottom. "*Oof!* That was graceful."

Captain Penelopeia grabbed Maia under her arm and pulled her in close. "I told you to hide in the queen's tent. Why did you not listen? Fool!" The captain released her after shaking her once or twice more than Maia felt warranted. She stumbled backwards but kept on her feet, supported by the mass of chanting Amazons.

Grunting, Maia marched back to Captain Penelopeia. "I *did* listen! Marpe knocked me out and brought me to two of Heracles's men. So take it easy with the shaking and pushing!"

"Marpe?" repeated Queen Hippolyta, pushing Captain Penelopeia aside ever so delicately. "Her treachery has no limits. And tell me, child, how did you escape?"

"I followed her," recounted Uncle Dorian, easing his way through the crowd. Pantariste lifted her spear, but Captain Penelopeia knocked it away with her sword. "Thank you, captain. I am pleased to see you alive, Queen Hippolyta."

"And I pleased to see you, son of Rhea. I am grateful as well for your rescue of young Maia."

"She is my family, Queen Hippolyta," said Uncle Dorian, placing his hand on Maia's shoulder. "How many of your sisters were lost?"

"Too many. Your nephew rides through Olympia unchecked, bringing ruin to all that remains. His quarrel with the Amazons is merely a distraction. After my near-fatal encounter with him, Heracles no longer sees me as a worthy opponent. He seeks... " Queen Hippolyta trailed off, her purple eyes resting on Maia. "He seeks the girl. Maia, I underestimated your account of the soldier in your home and his warning to you. Heracles seeks a combatant."

Pantariste snorted, further reminding Maia of a canine. "Do not mock the queen!" shouted Captain Penelopeia before striking Pantariste to the ground. The guard got up immediately, her face reddened. (Maia hadn't thought Pantariste was capable of displaying anything remotely resembling an emotion, especially shame.)

"Forgive me, my queen. But this child is barely off her mother's breast. How could Heracles seek to oppose her?"

"That is not for your understanding! Leave us. Tell your sisters to return to their responsibilities," ordered Captain Penelopeia. Pantariste bowed before lunging into the crowd and barking commands. "My queen, perhaps we should continue this dialogue in privacy."

"Quite right, captain. Our sisters have earned the privilege of ignorance in this matter," Queen Hippolyta said, "at least for now. It will not be long before they are called upon to raise their swords again."

* * *

UNCLE DORIAN LIFTED a double-headed ax from amongst a pile of weapons in Queen Hippolyta's tent. Running his fingers along the blade, he jerked his hand back exposing a slice on his index finger. Uncle Dorian put the tip of his finger in his mouth and sucked off the blood. "An impressive weapon," he said, examining his cut. "But it is nothing compared to a trident."

"Says the fool licking his wounds," said Captain Penelopeia, pursing her lips. "The labrys is the weapon of a warrior. A trident is good for little more than spearing fish."

"Had I not left my trident in the possession of my son, I would show you how wrong you are," countered Uncle Dorian, dropping the labrys. "I was distressed to learn of your city's destruction, Queen Hippolyta. The Amazons suffer greatly at the hands of Heracles."

"Thank you, Dorian, but when this is through my sisters and I will return to Pontus to restore glory to our home. And what are your intentions? Will Triton keep your seat of power, or will you seek to recapture your place in the pantheon?"

"Ha! How would I do that, your highness? I am no more a god than you. Even with Zeus's death, there is no means of restoring what once was mine. I sacrificed my birthright to assist in the creation of this world. That cannot be undone."

"A shame, really," said Queen Hippolyta, "especially if your restoration resulted in the undoing of Olympia."

"Am I hearing you correctly, your majesty?" asked Uncle Dorian. "Are you amongst those who favor the rejoining of our worlds? No. It may have taken me centuries to come to this opinion, but our kind cannot return to the homeworld. It would be ruinous!"

"Then we stay here and die. But now we know that you have managed to live amongst the homeworlders without calamity. How is that possible?"

"I have had assistance."

"From who?" asked Queen Hippolyta, coming within inches of Uncle Dorian. "Maia's father was to be the emissary, and we know his fate. Who else did Zeus send?"

"Can we stop this?" interrupted Maia. "Why does it matter? We're supposed to be talking about me and Heracles!" Maia looked back and forth between Uncle Dorian and Queen Hippolyta, but their eyes were locked on each other. "Ugh!" Maia exclaimed as she sat on the ground. "I can't believe you're both—"

"Hold your tongue, Maia. I will have answers from your 'uncle.' If you are to persuade me that the rejoining is a mistake, then you cannot hold back, Dorian. Zeus sent more than two of you," posed Queen Hippolyta. "All this time, it was believed that Stelios made the journey alone. If Zeus chose you to go with him, then... Hera! That is correct, is it not? By Olympus, Hera traveled with you to the homeworld!"

Uncle Dorian's silence was deafening. Maia studied him for some sign confirming Queen Hippolyta's assertion, but he remained as still as a statue of his former self. The longer she stared, the harder the realization came that she knew exactly who Hera was!

"Hera became my grandmother!" Maia exclaimed, picturing the small but forceful old woman she'd come to love three years prior. Yaya was the queen of the gods!

"Is this true, Dorian? Did you and Hera impersonate family in the homeworld?" asked Queen Hippolyta.

"We *are* family," answered Uncle Dorian, at last breaking his silence. "But yes, Maia's father and I 'posed' as brothers, and Hera as our mother. We used an enchantment – furnished by the witch Circe – to assume a place in a family consisting of a widower and his four sons. Hera and I were to assist Stelios, or Matthias as he called himself, in his mission."

"Zeus cast his own wife out of Olympia. Robbing her of her place amongst the gods was not devastating enough? Cruelty, thy name is Zeus," said Queen Hippolyta, slamming her staff into the ground.

"He did it as an act of kindness! Hera suffered deeply from her blight in Olympia. Zeus sent her to the homeworld to give her a chance at peace. And he was successful in doing so. Hera, goddess of women and marriage, treasured her new life. She loved the man she called her husband and all of his sons. Can you not see? Zeus did not cast her out – he freed her."

"Uncle Dorian, you told me once that Yaya didn't remember about Olympia," said Maia.

"This is true. Whether as a consequence of the enchantment we used or by her choice, Hera does not remember her former life. Though she lost her husband, she is surrounded by her sons and grandchildren and more than enough family to keep her content."

"That almost makes me think slightly better of Zeus," said Queen Hippolyta. "Almost. And it gives me more reason to think joining Olympia with the homeworld is a viable enterprise."

"Why? Because Hera and I have been able to 'blend in'? Where exactly do you propose hiding a tribe of satyrs? I know! Perhaps Circe could operate a veterinary clinic. And there would no longer be a need for airplanes. Everyone could travel on winged horses!"

"Even though I am not familiar with airplanes or veterinary clinics, I am fairly certain you are mocking me. Dorian, I am happy for Hera, and for you. But Zeus doomed us all when he made Olympia," said Queen Hippolyta, slashing the dirt with her staff. "Were it possible to save even a few of my sisters, I would advocate to bring the worlds together. Which brings us to Maia. Child, I do thank you for returning. Marpe will pay a dear price when—"

"She's dead. Heracles's men killed her," Maia interrupted.

Queen Hippolyta sighed, her shoulders falling. "Marpe *did* pay a dear price for her treason. All the more reason for you to leave."

"Leave? No, I'm staying. Dorian is taking me to see my father, and then I'm helping you to end this!"

"End what, child?" asked Captain Penelopeia. "This is not about some promise your father made. If the queen is correct—"

"Ahem!"

"That is, the queen, in all her wisdom, has deduced that Heracles wants to see you on the battlefield. Heracles will chase you to the ends of Olympia," said Captain Penelopeia. "Go home to your mother. There is no reason for you to die."

"But—"

"I told you, Maia. This was a foolish decision," said Uncle Dorian. "You cannot possibly fight Heracles. If you wish to see your father—"

"Heracles sent one of his men to contact me, so I'm no safer at home than I am here. Please, Queen Hippolyta. Yesterday, you offered to train me. Whether I stay here or go home, I need to be able to protect myself against Heracles."

Maia waited for the queen to answer. After several seconds, Queen Hippolyta rose and glided over to Maia, grabbing her by the chin. Slowly her grimace turned to a smile. Queen Hippolyta released Maia, picked up a sword, and put it in her hand.

"Captain Penelopeia, are you prepared to – what was it again, child? – be knocked on your ass?" asked Queen Hippolyta.

"Of course, my queen. I welcome the opportunity to 'kiss the dirt,' as it were. Today is as good a day as any to pay tribute to Gaia."

Maia reached down and with her free hand picked up the labrys Uncle Dorian had discarded. "Show me everything!"

CHAPTER 22

CRY 'HAVOC'

THE LEAD HORSE PIVOTED to the right, and Maia's horse followed. Though she liked pretending that she was in control, Maia conceded she was at the mercy of the magnificent steed. Xenophon was the color of a burning ember and every bit as hazardous. Maia leaned in and pulled on Xenophon's throatlatch by mistake, causing the horse to emit a cry that surprised Maia into letting go. She reached for the reins, but at the speed she was traveling the leather straps slipped out of her reach. Xenophon bore left, and Maia slid in the opposite direction, bouncing out of her saddle. As Maia braced for a fall, Captain Penelopeia sidled up to Xenophon on her ebony stallion, Harpagos, and grabbed Maia's ankle.

"How many times is this, adéxios?" taunted the captain. "By the will of the gods, I pray I remain close to you on the battlefield."

"Much as I enjoy your tough love – *oof!* – can you PICK ME UP?" cried Maia.

"*Heeya!*" shouted Captain Penelopeia, swinging Maia back on top of Xenophon. "Grab the reins!" Maia opened her mouth to thank the captain, but she was gone before she could utter a sound. Maia grit her teeth. Not far ahead was the target – a dummy crafted from hay and men's armor. Maia wrapped the reins around her left hand while reaching for her sword with her right. Xenophon picked up speed, eager himself to reach the end of this exercise.

"*Whoa!* Easy, boy! We're almost there," cried Maia as she pulled her sword free. Her breath was so heavy that she missed hearing the first twangs of bowstrings to her right. "*Heeya!*" Maia cried, applying pressure to Xenophon to swerve left even as she swung her sword. Two arrows whizzed by her head, but most fell to the ground, sliced in pieces by Maia's blade.

"Alala!" yelled Bremusa as she passed Maia. "You honor the daughter of Polemos!"

Bolstered by the Amazon's praise, Maia pulled Xenophon's reins, bringing her closer to the target. She raised her sword and struck, liberating the dummy's head from the rest of its body. Xenophon slowed of his own accord, which suited Maia as she struggled for normal breathing. When the horse stopped, Maia leaned forward and rested her head on Xenophon's chocolate-brown mane. "Good – *huff* – boy. That's a – *huff* – good horsey."

"Well done, Maia!" shouted Bremusa as she ran to Maia's side.

"Sorry – *huff* – about your arrows," Maia said, raising the corner of her upper lip. Maia gingerly lifted her head, pulling stray strands of Xenophon's mane from her mouth. "Was that necessary?"

"Ha! Comus, god of merrymaking, dost live in you, Maia!" said Bremusa, chuckling. "On the battlefield, you can expect much more in the way of obstacles than a few arrows, especially when you face Heracles."

"My niece does possess a great wit, does she not?" asked Uncle Dorian as he came up alongside Maia atop a shimmering white horse with eyes as blue as the Aegean Sea.

"We're still going with the whole 'uncle' and 'niece' thing?" Maia asked, arching her back until a shock of pain caused her to pull forward. "It's cute and all, but... " Maia began. She looked at Uncle

Dorian, who returned her gaze with narrowed, wrathful eyes, causing her to trail off.

"Your father was my brother in every sense of the word. As long as I breathe, you will be my niece." Uncle Dorian pulled on his horse's reins, and the animal pulled away like a bolt of white lightning. Maia rubbed her forehead and let out a long, exaggerated sigh. Guilt marched up her neck onto her face as Uncle Dorian disappeared over a hill. He didn't deserve to be on the receiving end of her sarcasm.

In the distance, Captain Penelopeia was giving commands to the other Amazons on horseback. Maia dismounted Xenophon. She returned her sword to its sheath as Captain Penelopeia neared. "So?" Maia asked. "Did I do good or did *I* do good?"

"That was skillfully done, adéxios," the captain said as she bounded off Harpagos. "I may need to find you a new appellation." Captain Penelopeia reached down and picked up the dummy's head.

"Yeah, a nickname other than 'clumsy' maybe? It doesn't inspire much confidence from the others," muttered Maia. She lifted her helmet and held it in front of her. Maia's jaw dropped at finding an arrow sticking through the horsehair crest. "Then again... "

"Better in your crest than in your neck," said Captain Penelopeia, the corners of her mouth nearly reaching her ears. "I am proud of you, Maia," she said, tossing the dummy's head at Maia's feet. "You may be an Amazon yet."

"Thanks," Maia said, pleased with the captain's praise but distracted nonetheless by Uncle Dorian's exit. Xenophon whinnied and prodded Maia with his head. With her free hand, Maia scratched under his chin groove.

"What troubles you?" asked Bremusa, pulling the arrow from Maia's helmet. "You have achieved a great deal these past days. Bare some pride."

"Especially considering that your fighting experience up until now has been with... a 'lacrosse stick,' you called it?" said Captain Penelopeia.

"Yeah, I've learned a lot... except for how not to bite the hand that feeds you," Maia said, stroking Xenophon's forehead.

"What do you mean? Who have you bitten?" demanded Bremusa.

"No, that's just... never mind, Bremusa. Thank you," Maia added. "As always, I appreciate your kindness. Excuse me, Captain Penelopeia, but may I go look for my uncle?"

"I believe you have earned a respite. Meet back at the olive tree grove before Helios approaches the end of his ride," said the captain. "Come, Bremusa, before Maia bites one of us."

"But what manner of bizarre dialogue is this?" Bremusa could be heard to ask as Maia galloped off on Xenophon. She hoped Uncle Dorian hadn't gotten too far. Cresting the hill where she'd last seen him, Xenophon's hooves began a steady clip-clopping as Maia spied a white horse with its head lowered, drinking from a stream. Uncle Dorian was nowhere to be seen. Maia pulled Xenophon in the direction of the watercourse, which seemed to agree with the animal. As the horse came to a stop, Maia bounded off – in her best impersonation of Captain Penelopeia – and landed in the stream. "Real smooth, adéxios."

Xenophon slurped up the water, inspiring Maia to do the same. After many gulps, Maia wiped her hands on her tunic and turned her attention to Uncle Dorian's steed. Tiptoeing, she approached the white horse from its side, to avoid the front blind spot as she'd been taught. "Hey there, snowy. Nice horse." The horse lifted its head, and Maia held out her hand for it to smell. "Yeah, that's right. What a beautiful boy... or girl... not gonna look... you're entitled to your privacy." The horse sniffed the back of Maia's hand and shook its head playfully. Maia moved to the horse's shoulder, nuzzling its neck. "Where's your rider, snowy?"

The quiet was broken as Xenophon whinnied and stamped his feet. A swirl of bubbles churned in the middle of the stream, growing wider and wider. Maia pulled her sword and gripped it with both hands, but she let them drop when Uncle Dorian emerged from the whirlpool.

Maia splashed the tip of her sword in the stream. "How deep is this thing?"

"Deep enough," Uncle Dorian answered, trudging through the water. "What do you want?"

"I came to apologize. That wasn't fair, what I said. You've been—"

"Deceitful? Secretive? Patronizing?"

Maia snickered. "Well, yes, all of those, but also understanding... and supportive. I'm sorry for doubting how you feel about me," Maia said, "but I keep having doubts about *everything*."

"Do you regret staying with the Amazons instead of first seeking out your father as you had originally intended?" asked Uncle Dorian.

"No, it's not that. You said he's not going anywhere, right?" Maia shook her head. "One minute, I feel brave and so sure of myself, and a minute later I'm wishing I was home with my mother."

"I believe that is called being a teenage girl. Your cousin Helena goes through the same torturous cycle," said Uncle Dorian, wiping water from his chin.

"Now that's patronizing. I think what I'm going through is a little more complicated than figuring out which pair of cutoff jeans to wear."

"Your burden is heavy. I do not mean to ridicule it. It is unfair that you are in this position. I also doubt my every action," said Uncle Dorian, "which is why I sought the counsel of my son. In giving up my throne, I also gave up the wisdom that comes with godhood. I see by your expression that you are puzzled. Maia, all bodies of water, even one as small as this stream, lead to the seas. Triton granted me an audience."

"And what wisdom did he share with you?" Maia asked.

"When Queen Hippolyta deems you ready, we must go to the garden of the Hesperides. This conflict with Heracles is fated to end in the far western corner of Olympia, at the edge of Oceanus," Uncle Dorian decreed. "It is an appropriate setting given the garden's place in the history of Olympia. The Great War began when Eris, goddess of discord, took an apple from the garden, thus sparking my vain sisters into a dispute that eventually encompassed the world. And it was too in the garden that—"

"Maia!" called Bremusa from the top of the hill. She jumped off a horse and sped down the knoll towards Maia and Uncle Dorian, skidding to a stop in a cloud of dust. Xenophon reared backwards on his hind legs and bellowed, spurring the "snowy" horse to jump into the stream.

"Forgive my interruption, but Queen Hippolyta commands your presence," Bremusa rattled off. "You must come at once!"

Maia raised her eyebrows at Uncle Dorian, and she was met with a smile. "You should go. Our issue is settled."

"You are to come as well, my lord," Bremusa added. "Queen Hippolyta asked for the honor of your company." Breathless, Bremusa bowed her head.

"Well, it does feel good to be wanted," said Uncle Dorian, "even without my trident. It would be my honor, of course." He stepped back into the stream and beckoned his horse.

"Bremusa, we'll be along shortly. Can you give us a moment?" Maia asked.

The Amazon nodded her head and ran up the hill to her horse. Giving a cry, Bremusa took off.

"What is it, Maia? I told you we are fine," said Uncle Dorian, climbing aboard his horse.

"Did Triton tell you anything else?" Maia asked, forcing herself to look Uncle Dorian in the eyes. Maia felt a lump in her throat as she acknowledged that she wouldn't be pleased with any answer.

Uncle Dorian stared past Maia, furthering her uneasiness. "My son gave me a warning – generous but not needed. If we fail to stop Heracles, his bloodlust will drive him beyond the confines of Olympia."

"He wants to go to my world."

"It is more than that. Heracles has discovered the means of permanently destroying the barrier Zeus created," Uncle Dorian revealed. "If not stopped, he will undo the creation of Olympia. He will rejoin our worlds."

Maia closed her eyes, scenes of destruction passing through her mind... Athens overrun by Heracles's men... the Eiffel Tower toppling to the ground... the U.S. Capitol Building in flames.

"And let slip the dogs of war."

CHAPTER 23

THE OATH

MAIA LOST COUNT of how many songs the Amazons had sung as the evening wore on into night. Wine flowed as steadily as the tears of a newborn baby hungry for a bottle. Even Captain Penelopeia took part in "honoring Dionysus" and paired up with Pantariste for one of the oddest duets in the history of song. The only participants sitting around the fire not drinking – other than Maia – were Queen Hippolyta and Uncle Dorian. They sat together for hours engaged in a discussion that kept them both riveted – and made Maia rather twisted.

Above the snapping flames, Queen Hippolyta let out a raucous laugh. "That's it!" Maia said. She scrambled to her feet, but the healer, Thais, blocked her path.

"The strength of one hundred men, thou dost possess!" slurred Thais. "You saved the queen!" Thais pulled Maia into a hug, the smell of grapes and sweat provoking an undesired screwing of her nose.

"You're welcome," Maia said, prying free. "It was the least I could do."

"You saved the queen!" Thais repeated, putting her hand on Maia's upper arm. "You saved the quee-ee-ee-eeen." Thais threw her head back and (to Maia's horror) began sobbing. Over Thais's shoulder, Maia saw that Queen Hippolyta and Uncle Dorian were no longer sitting by the fire. To where had they disappeared?

Thais let out a particularly grating shriek and fell to her knees, pulling Maia down with her. Maia wrenched her arm away and moved back towards the fire. There was no sign of the queen or her uncle anywhere between the singing and dancing Amazons. Amidst the chaotic celebration, Maia couldn't shake her agitation. Queen Hippolyta bizarrely commanded her presence and then ignored her, spending the evening canoodling with Uncle Dorian. Staring at the fire, Maia followed the zigzagging embers blown by the wind as the Amazons began a new song:

> *And Penthesilea did journey to Troy*
> *Twelve Amazons by her side*
> *A promise made to kill Achilles*
> *"For the glory of Troy," she cried*
>
> *Slay many Trojans, did she*
> *Before facing the massive Ajax*
> *With blood on her shield and sword*
> *She challenged him with an ax*
>
> *Ajax did cast her aside*
> *Scoffing at Penthesilea's might*
> *He sought out the warrior Achilles*
> *To enter and end the fight*
>
> *Penthesilea stood tall*
> *At Achilles's great strikes*
> *Alas, Penthesilea lost the battle*
> *And Achilles survived*
>
> *While mocking dead Penthesilea*
> *Achilles did look in her eyes*
> *Remorse filled his heart at last*
> *Over Penthesilea, Achilles cried*

"A sad tale, that of Penthesilea," said Queen Hippolyta, appearing next to Maia to her surprise. "Penthesilea believed she was destined to kill her queen. Gutted, she left our city in Pontus for Troy, prepared to die honorably in battle whilst also preventing my death." The queen wiped tears from her eyes. "Far too much of the history of our people is written in blood, Maia. You need to know this if you are to become one of us."

A wind blew through the campsite, peppering the night sky with embers. Uncle Dorian appeared by Queen Hippolyta's side. And then Captain Penelopeia joined them. The Amazons stopped singing and gathered around the fire.

"What's going on?" Maia asked, ice coursing through her veins despite the flames roaring behind her and the cinders dancing around her head like a swarm of fireflies.

"Maia, daughter of Stelios, are you prepared to take the oath of an Amazon?" asked Queen Hippolyta over the howling of the wind.

Maia's jaw shook uncontrollably. She swallowed several times before she was able to squeak out, "I am." Maia barely finished speaking when Captain Penelopeia advanced and placed a sword in Maia's hands. It was heavier than the one she'd been using and of finer quality. Maia squeezed the grip, and a charge surged through her, removing all traces of cold or doubt. She was meant to wield the sword.

"Kneel," Queen Hippolyta instructed. Once again, Maia looked to Uncle Dorian, and he gave an almost undetectable nod. Honoring the queen's command, Maia repeated the oath as it was spoken to her:

> *I will not bring dishonour on my sacred arms nor will*
> *I abandon my Amazon sisters. I will defend the rights*
> *of gods and all living creatures, and I will not leave*
> *my nation smaller when I die, but greater and better,*
> *so far as I am able by myself and with the help of my*

sisters. I will respect my queen and the existing
principles of the Amazons and all others established
by need. Furthermore, if anyone seeks to bring ruin to
our ways I will oppose this, so far as I am able by
myself and with the help of my sisters. Witnesses to
this shall be the gods... whomsoever do remain.

Maia's voice trembled as she recited the final words of the oath.
The wind stopped, and for a moment pure silence engulfed the
campsite like a thick fog. A fraction of an inch at a time, Maia
lifted her head, looking Queen Hippolyta in her kind purple eyes.

"You may rise, sister Amazon," the queen said, followed by an
explosive chorus of *"Alala! Alala! Alala!"*

Maia remained motionless until Pantariste broke through the
crowd, grabbed Maia under her arms and hoisted her into the air.
Maia collided into Uncle Dorian, and he put his arms around her
and hugged her tightly. "You have earned your place amongst the
Amazons, Maia," Uncle Dorian shouted over the screaming mass of
warriors. "Your father would be most proud."

Before Maia could respond to her uncle, Pantariste pulled her
away again, and Maia found herself surfing over the crowd of
Amazons. Her initial shock passed as speedily as she was passed
from Amazon to Amazon, and without realizing it, Maia was soon
laughing and crying with joy.

* * *

WHEN SHE FINALLY TOUCHED the ground again and was able to
break away from the celebration, Maia set out in the direction in
which she last saw Uncle Dorian headed. She came around a pair
of tents to find an empty lot. Maia refocused her attention on the

jubilant Amazons, curious as to when the festivities would end. Despite the noise coming from the bonfire, Maia picked up the familiar notes of a flute emanating from beyond a group of trees. Unlike the harmonics she was used to making in the school band, the instrument being played produced an odd, unearthly sound that was nonetheless compelling. Maia listened for several minutes before turning back to the party – and smacking right into Uncle Dorian.

"Easy, child. You may be an Amazon now, but you do not get to beat up every man that crosses your path. Actually, forget I said that. The queen is rather sensitive about the Amazons being portrayed as haters of men," said Uncle Dorian. "You must be overjoyed."

"Yes, I am, but it's still a lot to take in," Maia said. "This is what I wanted, and it feels right. Does it mean that I *have* to go after Heracles?" Maia pulled her newly gifted sword from its sheath. "When the time comes, will all of this training be enough?"

"You will not be alone, Maia. You are part of this tribe... of this nation of strong, brave women. You will never be without the backing of your sisters."

Maia lifted her sword, admiring the intricate etchings in the blade. A realization was triggered, and Maia shook her wrist, twisting her bracelet. Her sword matched the symbol that appeared on the bracelet weeks ago. "Uncle Dorian, look at—"

"I must leave, Maia. There are preparations I need to make to further our interests. Others need to be alerted to Heracles's plans," said Uncle Dorian.

"Where are you going? We're moving out in the morning. How will you find us?" Maia asked, thrusting her sword back into its sheath.

"I will find you the same way as I have always – with divine intervention. You will be fine, Maia. As I said, you are part of a sisterhood that will keep you safe. And you seem to be well practiced with your sword. I do hope that attack on your scabbard was not displaced for me."

Maia tilted her head. "No, it wasn't. But hurry back, please."

"I will return as swiftly as I am able," Uncle Dorian responded. He leaned forward and kissed Maia on the forehead. "Your mother would be proud as well."

"Now you're pushing it," said Maia, making no effort to cover up her smirk. She gave a short wave of her hand as Uncle Dorian withdrew.

"You have honored your family well, Maia," said Queen Hippolyta, catching Maia by surprise again as she scrambled for her sword. "Oh, do not be frightened, sister."

"Pardon me, your highness. But you're very good at sneaking up on people," said Maia.

"Yes, one of many qualities one must possess as queen. Ah, do you hear the flute playing of Pan? The god of the wild always did enjoy a bacchanal," said Queen Hippolyta. "Though he would be sensible to keep his distance!"

Immediately, the sound stopped. Maia heard a crunching noise in the distance, but wasn't certain it was anything more than the wind. A few seconds passed, and the notes began again, but from farther away.

"Some beings are so sensitive. I was merely trying to help him. Some of our sisters would rip him to pieces if given the chance," said the queen. "Too long a story to tell."

"I like the way it sounds when you say, 'our sisters.' I'm incredibly grateful for this honor, my queen," said Maia. "I promise not to disappoint you."

"It is well deserved, sister," Queen Hippolyta said, patting Maia on the shoulder. "Do not prostrate yourself so. Had you not earned the right to speak the oath, I shan't have granted you the opportunity to do so. You have made all of us, especially your queen, very proud. Captain Penelopeia too is on the verge of bursting."

"She didn't seem so proud when I almost fell off my horse this afternoon," Maia said. "Which makes it even harder to believe that I'm standing here, gifted with this sword."

"Do not be so mean, Maia. Perfection is impossibility, particularly in the short amount of time you have been amongst us. You devoted yourself completely to your training and though still capable of falling from a horse, you are also capable of greatness. There now, I take your smile as understanding."

"You... you remind me of my mother. That's the kind of thing she would say to me. 'As long as you try your best, that's all that matters.' She never cared if I won or lost or was first in my class. She was happy with the understanding that I gave my all." Maia's mind's eye was flooded with memories, both comforting and not, of occasions when her mother either applauded or scolded Maia depending on whether or not she could satisfactorily say she put everything out there. The final memory – her recent victory in lacrosse – caused a chill to spread through her body. Her mother beamed with pride when Maia lifted the trophy above her head.

"I take the comparison to your mother as the greatest of compliments. You describe a remarkably wise individual," said Queen Hippolyta. "She could be nothing but gratified with the daughter she raised."

Maia's face warmed. "Except she doesn't know anything about this. I should've told her the truth a long time ago. When Heracles is defeated and this is all over, I'm going to tell her everything."

Queen Hippolyta nodded. "Heracles will fall, Maia. Your mother will know of your triumph. You will have many rousing tales to recount. So many in fact that you can 'forget' to tell her about falling from your horse if you wish."

"Will Captain Penelopeia forget though? That's the real question."

"The captain boasted of your equestrian skills, Maia," Queen Hippolyta said.

"So, she'll officially retire 'adéxios' as my nickname?"

"I believe so," answered Queen Hippolyta, "but she still does on occasion call Pantariste 'the she-wolf.' Of course, I do not approve, even as feral as she was when I found her. Pantariste knew little but suffering until we took her in. It was not an easy transition. Once she understood that our love and support were unconditional, Pantariste set off on a path to being one of the greatest Amazons who has ever lived." Queen Hippolyta paused as the music from beyond the trees grew louder. "Pesky faun! He will regret it if he comes any closer."

"I guess I imagined that Pantariste had always been that way," said Maia.

"*Hmmm?* Oh, yes, she does strike quite an imposing figure. But she was weak and in need of refinement. The first time she rode a horse, I feared for all of our safety," Queen Hippolyta said with a laugh. "But why so serious, Maia?"

"I was thinking about Akantha. She turned her back on you after everything you did for her. She couldn't have been that much better off than Pantariste when you found her," said Maia.

"What is your question?"

"Pantariste's loyalty seems totally unbreakable. Why wasn't Akantha's allegiance equally as strong? Is her hatred for me so massive that she was willing to throw away everything she gained as an Amazon?" Maia asked.

"I do not have that answer, Maia. Akantha has chosen a different path. It will undoubtedly bring her ruination, but being an Amazon entitles one to self-determination. Do not think of Akantha. She has likely joined Marpe in the Underworld. Now, as your queen, I have a command – go to sleep. We break camp early in the morning."

"Yes, your highness," said Maia, bowing.

"Enough with the bowing," Queen Hippolyta said as she strode past Maia. After the sound of the queen's footstep withered, Maia pulled out her sword and swung it at the night air. It felt good. Maia thought about Queen Hippolyta's warning to Pan – if it was indeed the son of Hermes that continued to serenade her with his mysterious melody. He must've done something appalling to get the Amazons mad at him. And then to Maia's chagrin, the music stopped. It was better that way, Maia reckoned. She needed to try to sleep. Tomorrow the Amazons were beginning their march to Athens and to an inevitable collision with Heracles.

"Come and get me, son of Zeus. I won't 'idle' long."

CHAPTER 24

OUT OF THE SEA

XENOPHON MADE QUICK WORK of the streams and tributaries that marked the Amazons' path to Athens. Maia was pleased that they were staying close to the water. As always, the sea was a source of comfort, and she appreciated the pungent smell of brine and the squawking of seagulls even more so with the task ahead. Maia reached down and scratched her steed's neck. Xenophon was a beautiful horse, but all of the Amazons' horses paled in comparison to that of Queen Hippolyta. Lampus, as her name suggested, seemed to radiate light. When the Amazons set out that morning, Maia merely needed to look forward to see their route. Queen Hippolyta and her horse led the way like a lighthouse in a nor'easter.

In the distance, Pantariste circled the Amazons, keeping a watchful eye on the coming terrain. She looked healthier than Maia expected after the previous evening's merriment. With everything she'd seen Pantariste consume, Maia wagered she would have a hangover that could cripple her horse. Maia heard a clip-clopping noise from behind her, and she greeted Bremusa with a nod of her head as she pulled her horse up next to Xenophon.

"We have been favored with a beautiful day," said Bremusa. "How are you managing?"

"I'm okay," said Maia, reluctant to admit that the heat of the sun, though mild compared to recent days, was causing her armaments to double in weight. "Xenophon is giving me a very smooth ride, aren't you, boy?"

Xenophon snorted and shook his head, signifying to Maia that he didn't appreciate her babying. "Alright then."

"Do not embarrass Xenophon with Lampus nearby," Bremusa said with a laugh. "He is clearly drawn to her."

"Sorry, Xenophon. I didn't mean to cramp your style. You've got good taste though," Maia said, brushing Xenophon's mane. Bremusa chuckled, and Maia drew a long, content breath. She was glad for the distraction.

"Lampus was a gift to Queen Hippolyta from the goddess Eos," said Bremusa, her voice cracking. "Long did Lampus carry Eos across the arc of heaven to bring light to mortals and immortals alike. After the fall of Mount Olympus, Eos asked Queen Hippolyta to care for her."

"That must have been difficult for her – for Eos, I mean," said Maia, noting Bremusa's change in mood. Well ahead of them, Lampus carried Queen Hippolyta up a ridge. "And for Lampus too, I guess. It can't quite be the same."

Bremusa nodded. "Yes, though it does feel odd mustering sympathy for a goddess and her horse. The immortals had their way with our world for many centuries. Their fate was of their own design."

"I'm surprised to hear you say that, Bremusa," said Maia. "I thought the Amazons still held the gods in high regard."

"Having watched so many of my sisters cut down in battle, my faith has been tested. *Heeya!*" Bremusa cried before galloping off without warning.

Maia cringed at the thought that she'd offended Bremusa, but a murmur drifting through the convoy let her know otherwise. The Amazons closest to her slowed their horses, and Maia did the same. Xenophon snorted, and Maia realized her hands were shaking and thus pulling on the reins. "Sorry, boy," Maia whispered, the words nearly catching in her throat. She reached for her waterskin and fumbled with the wood plug, spilling water over her and Xenophon to the latter's annoyance. Maia gulped down the remaining water, but her throat kept as dry and rough as burlap.

At the lead, Queen Hippolyta sat gracefully atop Lampus, comforting Maia with her composure. Maia tied her waterskin to Xenophon's saddle, making eye contact with an auburn-haired Amazon as an arrow caught her in the shoulder. The Amazon grunted in pain. They were under attack!

"To arms, sisters! For the glory of our nation, Heracles's path of destruction ends on this day," cried Queen Hippolyta, rearing back on Lampus. From behind the queen, where moments ago there appeared to be nothing but barren fields, a storm of dust and smoke rose up from which emerged Heracles's army. Some of the attackers were on horseback, but many came charging on foot. Arrows filled the sky, and Maia, like those around her, raised her shield. *THUD! THUD! THUD!* Maia instantly lost count of how many arrows she blocked.

"Alala!" Maia cried after a moment of reprieve, squeezing her legs into Xenophon. Maia charged forward, pulling her sword. With a clearer view of Heracles's army, Maia saw that those on foot were not men by any natural sense. Their bodies were twisted and grotesque with animal limbs in place of arms. Some had more than one head, while others bore mottled wings.

"What the hell are they?" Maia shouted as a creature with the head of a cobra struck at Queen Hippolyta, only to be swatted like a mosquito denied its victim. The queen leapt from Lampus and drove her sword into the crossbreed. A swarm of creatures circled Queen Hippolyta. She patted Lampus on the shoulder and commanded, "Go!" Rearing back, Lampus took to the sky in a flash of light. Maia turned Xenophon in Queen Hippolyta's direction as the creatures engulfed her.

"No!" Maia screamed, clutching her sword until her entire arm shook. As she drew closer, Maia heard Queen Hippolyta laughing. Then and there, Captain Penelopeia blocked her path.

"Maia, the queen will fend for herself! Stay by my side. Heracles has yet to reveal himself," Captain Penelopeia yelled.

Maia followed Captain Penelopeia on her steed, Harpagos, matching her moves as close as possible. The captain cleared a swath through the battlefield, giving Maia few opportunities to test her sword. "Captain! Where are you taking me?"

"To safety!" Captain Penelopeia said as she discharged a creature of its two heads – one human and one of an elk. Before Maia could protest, the captain pulled back sharply on her reins, and Harpagos skidded to a stop. Something – or someone, Maia feared – had been thrown in their path. Xenophon still charged forward, hurdling over the impaled body of Pantariste cast so indelicately upon the ground. The harrowing sight caused Maia to slide off her horse and fall beside the fallen Amazon.

"Sister," Maia said through bated breath, reaching out to touch Pantariste. "Who could have done this to you?"

A ferocious snarling was Maia's sole warning that something was behind her. She yanked the sword from Pantariste's chest and wheeled around, slicing the claw-ended leg off a foul-smelling, hooded creature. It fell to the ground, and Maia stabbed the sword in its neck. Gasping, Maia fell forward and rested on her hands, battling the urge to be sick as her breakfast seemed to rise up from her stomach and take hold in her throat. Though Maia's vision was blurred, she could distinguish Captain Penelopeia running into sight. Maia coughed and wiped her mouth with the back of her hand, breathing a sigh of relief. The captain reached out to Maia – and was bashed aside, landing several yards away.

A pair of dark, hairy legs appeared in front of Maia. Straining to focus her eyes, Maia lifted her head, and an equally dark and hairy hand clutched her neck. Her keeper kneeled down, pulling Maia in close enough to touch foreheads. She could feel the man's fetid breath crawling over her face like a displaced colony of ants. His teeth were jagged and yellow, and when Maia struck up the courage to look at his eyes, she was staggered by their color – muddy violet spotted with pointed crimson flecks.

"Thou art yet more pitiful than I imagined," the man spat, tightening his grip. "I could kill you right now, as I did that virago," he added, motioning to Pantariste, "and put an end to this nonsense. But it will be a matter of time before boredom sets in again. Tell me, runt. When my father, Lord Zeus, gifted you that bracelet, did you actually believe it would keep you from harm?"

"Y-you?" Maia managed to sputter. "You're Heracles?"

"Yes, weakling. Look upon me. I may be the last thing you will ever see," Heracles taunted before releasing Maia. "Dost thou wish to challenge me? Dost thou dare raise your sword against the son of Zeus?" Heracles let out a vigorous laugh. "Do not shy away. Hippolyta's wenches have taught you the art of combat. FIGHT!"

Maia reached for her sword and held it shakily in front of Heracles. The demi-god roared with laughter, interrupting his gaiety only to scratch grossly underneath his tunic. Searching behind Heracles, Maia hastily surveyed the combat. The Amazons were holding steady, but Heracles's army of crossbreeds was pouring onto the battlefield from all directions. A steady stream headed directly for where Queen Hippolyta held her ground. She was making quick work of the monsters, but she couldn't advance due to the continuous onslaught. The queen wasn't yielding – and neither would Maia.

Maia fixed her sword. "Wh-what's the matter? Are you afraid of fighting the queen again? You know she would kick your ass this time!" Maia jeered, surprised by the words coming out of her mouth. "You set your dogs on her so you can pick on me. You're the pitiful one!"

Heracles's laughter came to a crashing halt. "Thou dares? I was going to have some fun, but you will meet my uncle Hades before I finish this—*Arghhh!*" Heracles toppled to the ground, an arrow jutting from his calf.

"Maia, run!" yelled Captain Penelopeia, limping towards Heracles with a bow in her hand. "Find Bremusa and stay by her side!"

Resistant to follow the captain's command, Maia took a step closer to Heracles. His agonizing screams let her know that it was no ordinary arrow that pierced his leg. Maia raised her sword. She could stop him from ever hurting someone else.

"Maia, behind you!" Captain Penelopeia screamed. Too late to turn around, Maia was tossed through the air. As she crashed into Pantariste's corpse, Maia lost her grip on her sword, and it landed out of her reach. A crossbreed jumped on her back, drooling saliva on her neck. Maia clawed the ground, grasping for Pantariste's sword, when the weight suddenly lifted off her.

"No, fiend! This one is mine," screeched a voice that Maia couldn't mistake. She rolled over and scowled to see Akantha holding a spear to the throat of a beast half-man, half-boar. The former princess showed no trace of regal bearing. Her voice may have sounded the same, but her overall demeanor was suggestive of the crossbreed standing beside her. "Take her!" Akantha barked, and the beast charged at Captain Penelopeia. "Do you like the animals, Maia? They were a gift from my mother."

Maia ignored Akantha, distracted by Captain Penelopeia's struggle with the crossbreed. She moved to help, but was immediately blocked by Akantha as she took up her customary ranting.

"Do not ignore me! I will have my vengeance for what you have done!"

"Get in line, princess! It seems like everyone wants to have at me," Maia shouted, gazing at Heracles still rocking on the ground. "At least let me get my sword."

"You get nothing, except for my spear in your throat!" cried Akantha. The disgraced princess charged, and Maia bolted after her sword. Spotting it a few yards away, Maia dove. As she seized the sword, Maia skidded over a short ledge and tumbled into a stream several feet below. Akantha balanced at the top of the ledge, her arm angled back to throw her spear.

"I have the high ground, Maia. Lay down your sword," Akantha snarled.

"Not a chance. You haven't managed to kill me so far. I have a feeling you'll screw it up again," Maia said, raising her sword.

"Do not mock me!" Akantha screeched as she released her spear. Maia struck out her sword, stabbing at the sky before bringing her weapon down. She sliced Akantha's spear inches from her face. The pieces of the spear fell into the stream, and Maia picked up the head.

"I think I'll keep this," Maia said, "you know, as a souvenir of your... what number is this? Is this the fourth time you've tried to kill me?"

"*AIIIIIIIIEEEEEEE!*" Akantha screamed as she pulled her shield from her back and jumped down from the ledge. Maia stuck her sword up and caught Akantha in the center of her shield. Akantha fell backward into the stream. She picked up the other end of her broken spear and waved it at Maia.

"Give up, Akantha. I don't want to kill you," Maia said.

"That is a shame because all I have dreamed about for three years is killing you!"

"Is this where you tell me again how I ruined your life?" Maia asked. "Yes, I know. I was responsible for your father's downfall. But you just mentioned a mother, right? She got those... 'things' for you? Say, your life can't be all bad."

"It is about to improve significantly," Akantha sneered as three of the crossbreeds jumped down from the ledge, surrounding Maia. She cut one with her sword, but was seized before taking any further action. "Do not eat her! Not yet, at least." Akantha waved at the crossbreeds to follow her up the ledge. Maia struggled to pull free, but the beasts were stronger than she could manage. Back on the field, Maia was pushed to her knees with her arms pulled behind her back. Her sword rested a few regrettable feet away.

"Do you see, Maia? The Amazons fight valiantly, but our forces are unstoppable. The queen will fall, and all of her sisters will follow," said Akantha.

"You were one of them. They took you in when you had nothing. How can you side with Heracles? He'll kill you just like his men killed Marpe!"

"No, Maia. Once this skirmish is over, I will be the leader. And perhaps Captain Penelopeia has already done me the favor of killing Heracles," Akantha said, searching their surroundings. "I do not see him or your horrid captain."

It was true. Though they'd been gone but a few minutes, Captain Penelopeia and Heracles were not to be seen. Akantha leaned forward and slapped Maia. Then she slapped her again.

Though her face stung, Maia looked at Akantha and said, "You're going to regret that."

"No, Maia. I will not," Akantha said, pulling her sword. "Good-bye."

BLLLAAATTT!!!

The mammoth blast of a trumpet rattled the battlefield, causing Akantha to stumble backward as she shifted her balance to stab Maia. An even louder blast cut through the air, and the crossbreeds released Maia as they howled in pain. Maia turned to the source of the noise. At the edge of the battlefield near the seashore, two cones of water shot up to the sky. And between them towered Triton, god of the sea, clutching his conch to his mouth. From the midst of the waterworks emerged Uncle Dorian. He turned around and yelled into the opening. Triton blew the conch again, and as the sound of the blast subsided it was followed by a rumbling that shook the battlefield even more vigorously.

"What witchery is this?" screeched Akantha, scrambling to her feet.

"You should know, witch," Maia said, kicking Akantha in the face. The former princess fell flat on her back and didn't move.

Out of the sea came a force of creatures Maia could scarcely grasp: squat men with the hindquarters of a goat she knew to be called satyrs, three-headed monsters with the tails of snakes breathing fire from each head, one-eyed giants, and to her dismay, gryphons – beasts with the bodies of lions and heads and wings of eagles. The creatures tore across the battlefield, tackling the crossbreeds. Screams unlike any Maia had ever heard sliced the sky as the monsters overtook each other.

"*Heeya!*" It was Alastor, the man Maia "met" in her living room. He charged her on horseback while swinging a flail – a weapon consisting of a spiked ball chained to a mace that Maia thought absurd during her training. Alastor neared her, and Maia raised her weapon. "You should have stayed home, girl," Alastor sneered. He raised the flail, but a shadow fell over him before he could strike, and a giant crushed him and his horse under its foot.

Maia stared up at the giant's one unblinking eye. "Thanks!" she said, sprinting across the battlefield to where her uncle held court.

"Uncle Dorian! How are you doing this?" Maia yelled over the furious swirling of the sea. Another giant emerged, and Maia waved as it stomped past her.

"It is not I, but my son Triton. His conch controls the beasts. He is doing his 'old man' a favor," Uncle Dorian said, unsuccessfully covering up a smile. Maia stepped forward and hugged him. "What was that for?"

"For believing in me," Maia said. "You may have screwed up a few times, but this makes up for it."

"Thank you, I think," said Uncle Dorian, hugging Maia back. "Where is the queen? And Captain Penelopeia?"

"I don't know. The queen was surrounded by a ton of those animals, but she seemed okay. And Captain Penelopeia shot Heracles with an arrow and then—"

"She shot Heracles? The son of Zeus is here?"

"He was. Then that crazy Akantha showed up, but I took care of her," Maia said.

Uncle Dorian looked back at the sea and whistled. Out of the whirlpool flew a winged horse of gleaming white. "I will fly over the fighting to locate the queen and captain. Stay near the water. You will be protected." Uncle Dorian climbed on the horse and to Maia's supreme jealousy, took to the sky.

With the seas swirling behind her, Maia planted her feet firmly in the ground. Triton's forces were easily overtaking the cross-breeds, freeing the Amazons to fight Heracles's men. Maia stabbed her sword into the sand and picked up a bow and a quiver of arrows. She wanted to rejoin the fight, but she knew her sisters were more than capable of soon ending the conflict. Still, Maia shot several arrows at Heracles's men, striking at least two. "MVP!" Maia shouted before cringing at her own smugness. Out of arrows, she flung the bow into the sand.

Then out of the chaos, Maia spotted Akantha limping her way. Her eyes were blackened, and her lip was swollen to twice its normal size. Good kick, Maia thought. Shrugging, Maia reached for her sword. But before Maia even picked it up, Akantha threw back her head and screamed as a gryphon swooped down and carried her away.

"Now you don't see that every day," Maia said as Akantha grew smaller and smaller over the horizon.

"Maia! Praise the queen, you live!" It was Bremusa, and she looked much worse for the wear compared to when they last spoke. She pulled Maia into an embrace. "Forget what I said earlier about the gods," Bremusa gushed, looking at the whirlpool. "We are blessed."

Maia hugged Bremusa tightly. They stepped apart, and Bremusa looked at Maia with a vast grin. She was smiling yet when a spearhead jabbed through her chest. Maia grabbed for Bremusa as she fell to her knees. Heracles came into view over the fallen Amazon's shoulders. He was pulling Captain Penelopeia by her hair. Releasing the captain, Heracles charged forward and yanked the spear from Bremusa.

"Shall we continue where we left off?" Heracles taunted, grabbing Maia by the arm. Pain shot through each of her fingertips.

"*KEEEEEEARRR!*" The cry of a bird of prey rang through the air over their heads as Uncle Dorian dove down on the winged horse. "Enough, nephew. Leave the girl alone."

"You call her a simple 'girl'? But Poseidon, you of all know that she is so much more than that," Heracles said. He pulled Maia in close, wrapping his arm around her neck. "I will kill her right now unless you give me what I want."

"And what is that, nephew? What could I possibly give you that you do not already possess?" asked Uncle Dorian.

"Passage to the garden of the Hesperides. It eludes me for reasons I do not understand. You will tell Triton to give me entry," ordered Heracles, squeezing Maia's neck. "But you balk. What is it that you know?"

"It is nothing. I will ask Triton to open the sea to you, once you release the girl," said Uncle Dorian.

"When we are in the garden," Heracles countered.

"Very well," said Uncle Dorian. "Let this bedlam end where it started."

CHAPTER 25

THE GARDEN OF THE HESPERIDES

WHILE BEING HURLED THROUGH a whirlpool into a long, winding tunnel of water was hardly the strangest thing that had happened to Maia since she discovered her connection to the gods of Olympus, it didn't make the experience any more pleasant. With every turn, Maia was convinced that she was going to drown. Somewhere in the tunnel with her was Heracles, and though she didn't understand why he wanted to take her to the garden of the Hesperides, Maia knew she had to make a stand, especially if Uncle Dorian wasn't able to follow. Maia was angry at his lack of resistance to Heracles's demands until she recalled that Triton had forewarned that the garden was where the conflict with Heracles would end. Still, as the tunnel narrowed and darkened, Maia wished Uncle Dorian hadn't left her alone with an insane demigod.

The water around Maia turned black, a small pinhole the sole source of light. Holding her breath, Maia reached for the light and was launched out of a decaying fountain onto a weed-ridden meadow. Tumbling across the ground, Maia sucked in a mouthful of rotted wildflowers.

"*Kaff! Kaff!* Ugh, that's gross!" Maia spat. Pulling a brown petal from between her teeth, Maia scanned her surroundings. The fountain of inky water and field of ill-tasting wildflowers shared their space with barren fruit trees and smoldering craters. "This is a garden?"

The fountain rattled, and Heracles came soaring out. He rolled on the ground much more gracefully than Maia and was on his feet instantly, bearing an insidious grin that sent ripples up Maia's arms.

"*Ha ha ha ha haaah!* This is what remains of the prized garden of Hera? My father's whore was more pathetic than I had known," bellowed Heracles, ignoring Maia for the moment. Without her weapons, Maia didn't see the point in attacking. But while Heracles was occupied with mocking and calling her grandmother names, she could attempt an escape. Maia put one foot behind her and then another, aiming to dive into the grove of unfruitful trees. As she turned her back to Heracles, a flash of light whizzed over her head, and a throng of trees were destroyed in an explosion of splinters and bark.

"Do not move, girl," shouted Heracles, "for I will not hesitate to use my father's thunderbolt to reduce you to ash. I had to pry it from his lifeless hands, but I am certain he would have wanted me to have his mightiest tool." Heracles threw his hands up. Lightning zigzagged down from the sky to his fingertips, and Heracles redirected the energy at the fountain, which disintegrated into a pile of rocks. "We cannot have anyone bothering us now, can we?"

A bolt of lightning struck the ground inches away from Maia's feet. She jumped back as another bolt blasted a mound of dirt by her side. With each detonation, Heracles laughed harder. He was playing with her.

"If you're going to kill me, do it already!" Maia yelled, fighting back tears. There was no way for her to defeat Heracles. "You have me where you want me."

"You? I do not want *you*. This was never about you. I want your father. I want to finish what we started centuries ago, before he became my father's ambassador and ultimately his greatest failure," said Heracles. "Stupid child. Did you really think the son of Zeus would waste his time with a weak pup such as yourself? If I do kill you, it will be because your father gives me no alternative."

"My father is here? He's in this garden?" Maia asked as her eyes darted around.

"Of course he is, idiot. He is where my father placed him after his betrayal. He stands in the same spot where he strained for millennia to prevent the heavens from crashing into Gaia," Heracles growled. Noting Maia's confusion, he pointed to the edge of the garden. "There, you simpleton. Allow Heracles to show you." Heracles rubbed his hands together, electricity crackling around his knuckles. Pulling his hands apart, he unleashed a bolt of lightning ten times the power of the one he used to destroy the fountain. The lightning hit a previously unseen target, wrapping itself around the figure of a man holding an orb of incalculable size.

Maia stumbled forward. It made no sense. How could that man be her father? Before she could think on it any further, Heracles hurled a succession of bolts at the man. He didn't move. But then, he didn't seem alive. He couldn't be alive, Maia reasoned.

"He is tenacious, I will admit. None but Medusa herself could produce a better statue – if I had not killed her, of course," Heracles said before erupting into a fit of laughter. Maia liked him even less when he was charmed by his own doing. Heracles was still laughing when a jet of water burst like a geyser from the pile of rocks where the fountain had flowed. From out of the torrent emerged Uncle Dorian. He was holding a trident like a child who found a long-lost toy under his bed. Uncle Dorian proudly brandished his weapon, filling Maia with hope.

"This is over, Heracles. Stand down and I will let you live," declared Uncle Dorian.

"Because you hold your trident, you mean to intimidate me? Be gone!" Heracles cried as he fired a bolt of lightning at Uncle Dorian. The lightning struck the trident, but Uncle Dorian twisted it around, sending the lightning back at Heracles. Unprepared, Heracles was thrown to the ground. His sword came loose from its sheath and landed near Maia.

"You remember some of your tricks, I see. But you are not a god. You are nothing," Heracles spat as he charged Uncle Dorian. Maia hoped that Uncle Dorian could fend off the attack, but Heracles knocked him aside. For all of Uncle Dorian's bravado, the son of Zeus was right – he was just a man and about as big a physical threat to Heracles as was Maia. Heracles picked up the trident and held it to Uncle Dorian's throat.

"It was good of Triton to return this to you. It is a fitting means to end your life," Heracles said. "Or do you wish to watch me end another life before I kill you? You can keep the girl company."

Her head buzzing from all of the activity surrounding her, Maia scarcely heard the arrow as it zipped down from the sky, catching Heracles in the shoulder. "*Arghhh!*" the demi-god cried, clutching the arrow.

Queen Hippolyta swooped down riding Lampus, flying as easily as if the horse had wings. She jumped on top of Heracles, pushing the arrow deeper into his shoulder amidst his screams.

"Feel the poison course through your veins, Heracles! Let your last vision be my face. You are fin—" Queen Hippolyta began before Heracles reeled around and blasted her in the chest with a bolt of lightning. She landed on her back with her eyes closed, not far from Uncle Dorian.

"I felt the poison before, when your captain attempted the same tact. Painful at first, yes, but the lightning burns it away. Did that surprise you?" Heracles said, placing his foot on Queen Hippolyta's throat. "Tell me, child. What do you think of your queen now?" Heracles asked, pulling the arrow from his shoulder.

Maia prayed Queen Hippolyta was alive. But more than that, she raged at seeing Heracles hurt someone else she loved. Maia picked up Heracles's sword. "I think she's stronger than you'll ever be. And I think you should get your mangy foot off her and come fight me!"

A growl rising through her throat, Maia raised the sword and shifted her feet to charge Heracles. But before she could take a step, someone pulled her arm back. Spinning around, Maia looked into the eyes of a man she recalled seeing in pictures but never in life – her father.

"Leave him to me."

"Ha! He lives!" Heracles cried. "Atlas lives!"

Maia dropped the sword. "Dad? Is it really you?" Maia asked, her chin trembling like the waters of a pond in a windstorm.

"Maia? You are my daughter Maia? But what are you doing here? How did—"

"Pardon the intrusion," interrupted Heracles, "but I would like to get on with killing one or both of you. You can continue your reunion on Charon's boat."

"What manner of insanity have you wrought, Heracles? How dare you threaten my daughter? I accepted the punishment Zeus handed down to ensure the safety of my wife and child. Who gave you the right to break that covenant?" Atlas boomed, pushing Maia behind him. "Leave this place!"

"Who gives me the 'right'? Who gives Heracles the 'right'?!? Zeus is dead. The gods of Olympus are no more! I rule this world, and I will do as I please!"

"And what do your delusions of grandeur mean for me and my daughter?"

"You? You are unfinished business. Oh, mighty Atlas, you supported the heavens themselves on your shoulders for millennia. But was that your greatest feat? No. Once you gave up your post, your notoriety grew, though few knew whom you really were. Zotikoz? Teris? Stelios? You drifted through Olympia, a hero to many and a friend to every being you encountered. All while I suffered."

"What stupidity is this, Heracles? What did my freedom have to do with your suffering?" asked Atlas.

"The apples! They were poisoned. After I left the garden with the apples you so kindly fetched for me, I journeyed to the Underworld to complete my final labour. Before I was to capture Cerberus, my uncle's three-headed hound, I ate one of the apples. As soon as I bit into it, I knew you had poisoned it. And in the Underworld I remained until freed by the squabbling on Mount Olympus wrought by the Great War. You cursed me to centuries of torture! And now I will have my vengeance."

"You are truly mad, Heracles. I did not poison the apples I secured for you," said Atlas.

"Do not continue your deceit!"

"Heracles, how many others sought to prevent you from completing the tasks King Eurystheus set before you? Any number of individuals would have poisoned you to keep you from atoning for the sin of killing your wife and children – and the sins you committed in completing your labours, for that matter. No, Heracles, I did not poison you, but I will not hesitate to end your crazed existence if you threaten my daughter again."

"No, it had to be you! I killed all the others, except for that witch," Heracles said, pointing at Queen Hippolyta. "I killed everyone involved in my labours, including King Eurystheus. All of them denied betraying me. You are the last."

"And I deny your asinine accusation as well. It is not vengeance you seek but distraction. You use your stint in the Underworld as an excuse to carry out your villainous ways. But Heracles, you are free! Only I understand better the glory of freedom. Forget the time you spent in the Underworld and defy your fate. You are liberated," said Atlas, "and I intend to remain so as well."

"No, Atlas. I used my father's lightning to free you for one reason – to watch you die. And then, after I kill your daughter, I will tear down the barrier surrounding Olympia, and I will conquer the homeworld as well."

Atlas picked up Heracles's sword. "I will not stand for that."

"That is what I hoped for," said Heracles, his mouth twisted in a wrathful smile. He swaggered over to Queen Hippolyta and seized her sword. "I will have my weapon back."

"From my lifeless hands," said Atlas.

"So be it," Heracles taunted.

"No! What are you doing? He'll kill you!" said Maia, grabbing her father's sleeve. "Let's just get out of here."

"Maia, you know I cannot allow him to leave Olympia," said Atlas, stroking the side of Maia's face. "You have grown into a beautiful young woman in my absence. And I intend to watch you grow further."

Atlas pushed Maia away as Heracles charged. Heracles struck first. Atlas countered, but it was apparent from the start that Heracles was stronger. Lightning crackling around them, Heracles blocked blow after blow, as did Atlas, and they may well have continued in this way had Heracles's own sword not shattered in Atlas's hands.

"I knew that piece of excrement would give. It has been cracked since I beheaded Eurystheus sitting on his throne. And so it ends, Atlas. After your daughter watches you die, I will take her life. The sea god will die as well, and the Amazon too – after I have my way with her. And when I journey to the homeworld, I will kill your wife. Then I will know peace," said Heracles. He slinked behind Atlas, keeping Queen Hippolyta's sword at his throat.

Beginning with her hands, Maia's entire body convulsed as if struck by Heracles's thunderbolt. She couldn't let her father die, not when she finally got him back. Maia winced from a shocking pain in her wrist. Her bracelet was melting! Maia grasped for it, but the bracelet dripped through her fingers and fell to the ground, where it took the form of a thin but pointed sword.

"Goodbye, Atlas," Heracles said, tightening his grip. He curled his lips back in a sneer, and from between his teeth came a spray of blood. Cursing, the demi-god dropped Queen Hippolyta's sword. He brought his hand to his chest and touched the bloody tip of the golden sword Maia had driven into his back. Heracles fell sideways, his eyes wide with uncertainty. He reached for Maia, but Atlas pushed his hands away.

"Then fall, Heracles," the demi-god muttered as his eyes went dark. The son of Zeus was no more.

Maia threw the golden sword aside. Heracles's blood was on her hand. She had fulfilled her father's promise.

Atlas pulled Maia into his arms. "Are you okay?"

"I'm better," Maia answered as she wrapped her arms around her father. Tears streamed down her face. "I'm better than I've been in a long time."

Atlas rested his chin on Maia's bushy mane. "As am I, daughter. As am I."

CHAPTER 26

HOPE IN BLOOM

MAIA STROLLED THROUGH THE ORCHARD with her arms out, letting her fingertips touch the crusty, gray growth covering the lifeless tree trunks. A dragonfly buzzed in her ear, and Maia flinched. The insect flew over her head, and Maia followed its sharp twists and turns along the path running between the trees. She quickened her pace to keep up with the dragonfly, which stopped and hovered near a tree no taller than Maia's waist. Between the muted leaves, a glint of color revealed itself. Kneeling, Maia pushed the branches apart, joyously chuckling at her discovery of a glistening golden apple. There was life in the garden after all. The dragonfly hovered for another moment and darted into the sky.

The pointed snap of a branch warned Maia of someone's approach. She let the leaves fall back over the apple, silently wishing that it would be the first of many. Maia paused, comfortable in the belief that for the first time in a very long while the person behind her meant her no harm.

"What have you found, Maia?" her father asked, placing his hand on her shoulder.

Maia cupped her hand over his. "Hope," she answered.

"That is something your mother would say," Atlas shared. He let out a distinct breath. "How *is* your mother?"

"She's... okay," Maia replied, turning to face her father. "She never got over it."

"My disappearance."

"Yes. She was sad for a long time. And angry too," Maia said. "I didn't find out about you until three years ago. Mom never talked about Greece or your family." Maia paused. "She still thinks you abandoned us."

Atlas closed his eyes. "In a manner of speaking, I did. If I had handled my affairs differently perhaps... no, the outcome would have been the same. Zeus was furious with me and with Hera and Poseidon as well. He never intended for any of us to find happiness when we left Olympia. We were to observe and report back. Instead we established lives for ourselves. Hera found a loving family," Atlas continued, "and I found your mother. After you were born, I swore never to return to Olympia. I tried to keep the truth from your mother, but she knew something was wrong. Zeus sent for me, and I was not strong enough to fight. I pleaded for mercy, but Zeus set my fate. Daedalus, the artificer, had discovered the means of crossing the barrier between Olympia and the homeworld. In doing so, he weakened the barrier, and Zeus feared for the worst. My punishment was to reassume my place shouldering the heavens to give stability to Olympia."

"So, you're a god?"

"Ha! Well, I was a Titan to be exact. We came before the gods. But I am no more a god or Titan than Poseidon. I am a man. Zeus used the head of the gorgon Medusa to fix me in place, which gave me the strength to support the heavens. He could have done the same to anyone, but Zeus meant to punish me," Atlas said, taking Maia by the hand. "Nothing less than the merciless fury of the king of the gods could keep me from my wife and daughter."

Maia bit her lip to keep from crying again, but it was a futile effort. Atlas put his arm around her as they strolled through the orchard. Wiping her eyes, Maia asked, "How is Queen Hippolyta?"

"Poseidon, that is, Dorian believes she will be fine. I am sure she will not be happy that Heracles was able to defeat her, but it was not the first time. Events have a way—"

"Of repeating in Olympia," Maia finished. "I've heard that before. Which brings a question to mind. Did you have another daughter named Maia?"

"In a way of speaking, yes, but... no. I did not father the Pleiades as I fathered you. I 'assisted' in their creation in a primordial sense," Atlas explained. "Maia was my favorite. After her light was extinguished at the end of the Great War, I thought I would never see a soul as beautiful and pure – until you were born."

Maia and Atlas exited the orchard and entered the clearing with the remains of the fountain. Uncle Dorian sat atop an ebony winged horse, brandishing his trident. "Ah! There you are. Shall we take our leave?"

Atlas pulled Maia in closely. "We should depart this place."

"The Amazons have offered us refuge – your father and I, that is. You, Maia, are one of them," Uncle Dorian said with a bow.

"What about Heracles? What are you going to do with his, um, body?" Maia asked, the enormity of having killed the son of Zeus weighing on her.

"He will rest here in the garden of the Hesperides," Uncle Dorian answered, pointing to a mound of dirt, "until we have made certain that the queen and your sisters are well. Do not burden yourself, Maia. You acted as an Amazon. Your actions saved all of us – and preserved the barrier between Olympia and the homeworld."

"Maia, you are a hero."

"Yeah, tell that to my therapist," Maia muttered.

"I told you that your daughter possessed quite the wit," Uncle Dorian said.

"I promise you, Maia. I am not going anywhere, and I will help you with this burden," Atlas said, stroking Maia's hair in a way that reminded her of her mother. She was also safe because of Maia.

"I'm ready to go now," Maia said, squeezing her father's hand.

Atlas gazed around the garden that had long served as his prison. "Yes, well, as I once said to Zeus, let us get on with it."

* * *

XENOPHON TOOK ANOTHER CARROT from Maia. "Good boy," Maia said, scratching behind the horse's ear. "I'm gonna miss you, fella. You're the best horse I've ever been on – with or without wings." Xenophon whinnied. "Sorry, that was my last carrot." The horse stomped its forelegs. "Oh, come on, Xenophon, don't... " Maia began, but the horse trotted off. "Yeah, nice knowing you too," Maia said, shaking her head.

Maia picked up her sword and shield. Heracles had tossed them into the surf before forcing her to make the trip to the garden of the Hesperides, but Triton kept them safe. The question now was what to do with them. She could bring them when she left Olympia, or she could ask Captain Penelopeia to keep them for her. As she slid the sword into its sheath, Maia realized that the issue wasn't really about her armaments. Was she ready to go back to her old life? The same question had plagued her three years ago, and in the end she felt the need to return to Olympia. The emotions were different this time though, Maia pondered as she spied her father sitting with Queen Hippolyta. They were laughing. It was a welcome sight after the previous day's activities. The funeral pyre from last week was nothing compared to the inferno that consumed the bodies of the fallen Amazons, amongst them Pantariste and Bremusa.

"Ah, there she is," Queen Hippolyta said, holding out her hand. "I was just bragging to Stelios about your warrior skills."

"*Hmmm.* That is a name I have not heard for a very long time," Maia's father said, nodding his head.

"Forgive me, I did not even think to ask. Is there a name you prefer? Atlas, perhaps?" Queen Hippolyta asked.

"No, I am quite happy to relinquish my Titan name. Matthias will do. It is the name by which my wife knew me."

"Very well, Matthias. And you, Maia? What shall we call you?" asked Queen Hippolyta.

"I'm not sure what you mean," Maia answered, shrugging her shoulders.

"The mystery as to how you possess such strength has been solved," said Queen Hippolyta. "When we first spoke of your father, I chose not to disclose the rumors of his origination. It is always best to withhold uncertainties. I knew your father to possess great strength, but far stranger things are more common in Olympia than a man capable of uprooting a tree. Though it does raise a question... are you a Titan?"

"I d-don't know." Maia looked at her father. "Why *am* I so strong?"

"Your uncle and I have discussed this. You are a child of two worlds – the first of your kind. Though I did not possess my full capabilities when you were born, there could be residual energy that I passed to you," said Matthias. "The queen is joking, of course. This does not make you a Titan or even a demi-god. It is a gift you may use when you return to Olympia."

"And return you will, Maia," said Queen Hippolyta. "Olympia survives because of you. While Heracles is not the sole threat to peace, he was by far its greatest known challenger. There is wonder here to explore. It saddens me that your experiences thus far have been so brutal. Come back to us, Maia, and I will show why I believe the worlds should be rejoined."

"Do not start with that, your highness," said Uncle Dorian as he approached them. "If this series of events with Heracles should have taught you anything, it is that we are all better off with the way things are."

"Well, perhaps I am just a slow learner," said Queen Hippolyta, arching her eyebrows. She held out her hands to Maia. "Thank you, sister. May the gods protect you always." The queen nodded at Matthias and Uncle Dorian, and smiling once more at Maia, turned and headed in the direction of the healer's tent.

Queen Hippolyta disappeared into the tent, to check in on Captain Penelopeia and countless others, Maia presumed. "Oh! I forgot to ask the queen about my sword and shield."

"You may bring them with you," Uncle Dorian stated.

"Somehow I don't think they're going to let me take them on the airplane," Maia said.

"*Humph.* You will leave them with me in Greece, of course. I will keep them safe until you need them again," said Uncle Dorian. "And speaking of your safety, here is something for you." Uncle Dorian held out his hand. Resting in his palm was her bracelet. "I asked the blacksmith to remold the blade into its former shape."

"Will it work the way Zeus promised?" Maia asked, slipping the bracelet on her wrist.

Uncle Dorian shook his head. "I am not certain, but we cannot deny that it served you well in the garden of the Hesperides. Some enchantment clearly remains."

"Yes, clearly, since it morphed into a knife. Maybe Zeus isn't dead," Maia offered.

"Or someone else has taken over your guardianship," countered Uncle Dorian. "There is little reason to suspect that my brother lives."

"Why can't you ask Triton about the bracelet? And while you're at it, ask him how one of Heracles's men got into my house," said Maia.

"It does not work that way, Maia," Uncle Dorian said. "My son owes me no explanations. What information he has given me, I accept graciously. I will not quiz him unnecessarily."

"Dorian, what Maia asks of you is not unreasonable. I am disturbed to hear that one of Heracles's men was able to cross the barrier and travel so far from Greece," said Matthias. "You may think it trivial, but my daughter's safety is of the utmost importance. I will not allow her to be put in jeopardy."

"Matthias, those of Heracles's men who survive have been searched. None have the means of traveling to the homeworld. Maia can return to Sea Cliff without worry," Uncle Dorian declared.

"I know I'd feel much safer if you came with me, Dad."

Matthias cocked his head and smiled. "Maia, we have discussed this. I do not know if it is wise for me to show up and disrupt the life your mother has made for the two of you. I will make the journey from Olympia with you and Dorian. And in time, we will determine the best course of action. I will keep my promise to you, Maia. I will be there to support you in every way, even if I am not in Sea Cliff with you at first."

"Okay, but Mom has been waiting for fifteen years. That's long enough," Maia said. "When we cross over, where will we be?"

"We are not far from Athens," said Uncle Dorian. "You will be able to meet up with your ambassador group and travel home in two days."

"That doesn't seem like enough time," Maia said.

"Then we should stop talking and go now."

CHAPTER 27

ONLY THE BEGINNING

THE LOBBY OF THE ROYAL OLYMPIC HOTEL in Athens was overrun with teenagers in ill-fitting suits and skirts of questionable lengths. Maia paced near the revolving door searching the crowd for Jackie with little success. After several minutes, the leaders began calling out names. Maia spotted Nate, and she rushed over to him.

"Firecracker! You made it," Nate said, wrapping his arms around her. "How's your Grandma?"

"She's fine. Thanks for asking. Have you seen Jackie?"

Nate chuckled. "Check the couch over by the restaurant," he said, gesturing with his thumb over his shoulder.

"Couch?" Maia leaned to look around Nate. She saw an older, heavily painted woman standing at a podium stacking menus. The woman wore a sour expression on her face as she kept looking to her side. Two kids were sitting on a couch, their lips locked. "Whoa! Is that Jackie and Roc?"

"Yep," Nate said. "They got real close while you were gone. Say, are you coming to the closing ceremony?"

"Um, I'm not sure. I guess I should talk to one of the leaders. We got to Athens last night. I'm staying at the hotel across the street with my uncle," said Maia, moving so Nate blocked her view of the unwelcome public display of affection. "What time is the ceremony?"

"We're leaving in a few minutes for the Acropolis. I can't wait! Have you ever been there?"

"Three years ago when I came to Greece the first time. Nate, there's something I have to ask you about the last time we spoke."

"You mean the kiss? Sorry if I took liberties, but—"

"No, not the kiss. But for future reference, ask first. You said something about a helmet. What did you mean?" Maia asked. "Nate, I'm asking you a question. What do you keep looking at?"

"Sorry, Maia, it's just that there's two guys over there watching us. I mean, they're doing a pretty bad job of pretending that they're *not* watching us," Nate said, waving at Maia's father and uncle.

"What are you guys doing here?" Maia asked after Uncle Dorian and Matthias joined her and Nate. "You said you were going to stay at the hotel."

"Maia, are you going to introduce us to your friend," her father asked, looking Nate up and down. "What? Can a father not be protective?"

"This is your Dad? I thought you said he—"

"We just reconnected. It's a long story. Nate, this is my father and my Uncle Dorian."

"It is a pleasure, Nate," Matthias said, shaking the boy's hand. "You have to forgive me. I have many years to make up for."

"Understood, sir," Nate said. "But I don't think you have to worry about Maia. She seems to be able to take care of herself."

"Yes," Matthias said with a snicker. "I believe that she... um, I believe... "

"Dad, what is it?" Maia asked, following his eye line to the elevators. A bellboy pushing a luggage cart disappeared into an open elevator, revealing Maia's mother. She was looking through her purse, giving no sign that she'd seen Maia.

"What is she doing here?" Maia asked.

Uncle Dorian pursed his lips, but said nothing. Maia's father's face was drained of all color. She looked back at her mother just as she raised her head. Mrs. Peterson smiled as she put her hands on her hips. She mouthed, "Get over here," and Maia complied.

"Mom, what's going on?" Maia asked as she threw her arms around her. "How did you know I'd be here?"

"Dorian wrote to me. He sent me a letter with a ticket after I spoke to you last week. He insisted I come. The whole thing sounded crazy, but—oh, there he is!" Maia's mother said, waving at Uncle Dorian. "Who's that with... " Mrs. Peterson froze. In spite of the noise generated by the youth ambassadors, Maia swore she could hear her mother's heart pounding in her chest.

"Mom, I have to tell you... " Maia began, but it came as no surprise that her words were falling on deaf ears. She looked at her father and motioned for him to join them. He ambled across the lobby. Face to face, Maia's parents stared at each other. Her mother's expression was unreadable; her father's face revealed an uncomfortable mix of fear and joy. Maia could relate.

"Say something," Maia said to her father.

"Eleanor, I am so—"

"Don't speak. Maia, let's go," her mother said, grabbing Maia by the hand.

"Mom! No, wait."

"I said, let's go!"

"Eleanor, please—"

"No! I don't want to hear whatever it is you're going to say because there's nothing you *can* say to make up for the last fifteen years!" Maia's mother exclaimed.

A few youth ambassadors turned their heads, intrigued enough by the scene unfolding in their midst to interrupt their fun. Maia clasped her hands together and gave a pleading look, but her mother shook her head. "I'm leaving, Maia, and you're coming with me."

"Mom, he didn't want to leave."

"Stop it, Maia!" her mother snapped.

"Mom, it wasn't his choice. There's a lot I have to tell you," Maia said, her voice cracking as tears spilled down her face. "I should've told you what I found out about Dad when I was here three years ago, but—"

"Maia, what are you talking about?" her mother interrupted. "What did you find out? What lies did he tell you?"

"Eleanor, you cannot blame her. The secrets she was forced to keep would have been impossible for you to believe. Unless... Eleanor, do you remember the day we were married?"

"Of course I do. You don't forget the day you made the biggest mistake of your life."

"Do you remember what you saw in the sea as we looked down from the temple of Poseidon?" Matthias asked.

"What? Why are you bringing that up? You told me I just imagined it," Maia's mother answered.

"What was it?" Maia asked.

"Oh, it's stupid, Maia. Don't listen to him," her mother said as she frowned at Maia's father. "What's your point?"

"Mom?"

"Fine! There was a man with... oh, what do you call it? A trident. He was out in the middle of the water," Maia's mother said. "He was holding a trident in one hand and a giant shell in the other. This is ridiculous! It was just the heat getting to me."

"Mom, I've seen him too. His name is Triton. He's a god."

Maia's mother shook her head. "That's absurd."

"Mom, I know how it sounds, but you saw him! The gods are real... and they had Dad trapped for the last fifteen years," Maia said, lowering her voice. "You have to believe me."

Maia's mother stared at her for several seconds. "No, I can't. Even if I could accept—"

"Eleanor, could you possibly believe that I would leave you and our child willingly? You have done wonders raising her. Maia is everything I could have dreamed for in a daughter. But I never would have chosen to not be by your side."

Maia's mother's entire body shook. She looked at the floor, small, painful sounding huffs of air coming from her mouth.

"Eleanor, as I professed long ago beneath the stars on Cape Sounion, my heart is and always will be yours."

Maia's mother lifted her head, gasping for air. She bit her lip, her face wet with tears. And then, she smiled. "Matt... "

"Yes, Eleanor?"

"Matt, you stole that line from a movie," Maia's mother said, laughing through her tears.

"Oh, Eleanor," Matthias said, grabbing hold of her hands. "Please know that—"

"Just shut up and kiss me," Maia's mother interrupted.

"With pleasure," her father said, pulling her in for a long, deep kiss.

Maia wiped at her tears, but there was no quelling them. Her whole body went numb as Maia watched her parents' reunion. She felt a twinge of discomfort in her side, but it subsided – permanently, Maia supposed. She looked at Uncle Dorian. He nodded and backed away towards the revolving doors, exiting the hotel without a word.

Nate sidled up to Maia and put his arm around her. "Don't you just love a happy ending, firecracker?" he asked.

Maia rested her head on Nate's shoulder. "Yes, but this is only the beginning."

EPILOGUE I

ONE DAY AFTER THE CREATION OF OLYMPIA

LORD ZEUS LOOMED OVER a large basin filled with an ebony liquid. In the middle of the liquid, there appeared an image of a young man standing on a cliff holding a walking stick. The wind was blowing the man's mop of curly hair and simple clothing with a ferocity that threatened to knock him off the cliff, yet the man was grinning from ear to ear. Zeus reached for the basin, but pulled his hand away, sparks of electricity dancing on his fingertips.

"Brother, I will take my leave of you now."

Zeus turned away from the basin and looked upon his brother Hades, god of the Underworld. "Very well."

"You look upon Hera's scrying pool. Are you watching her?"

"No."

"Poseidon, then?"

"No. The one who calls himself Teris now – the former Atlas."

"He willingly gave up his being? Even after you freed him?"

Zeus sat on his throne. "Atlas's time shouldering the heavens had an unintended effect. It made him knowledgeable of ideas about existence that Lord Zeus himself does not understand. It made him desire humanity."

"He is a fool, brother," said Hades.

"Yes, but a happy one. You have Lord Zeus's gratitude for personally escorting Apollo to your realm."

"You are the king of the gods, brother, and as such your commands are mine to follow. Yet I have never heard you utter a word such as 'gratitude.' What has come over you?"

Zeus turned back to the basin. "Change."

EPILOGUE II

A CHANGE IN THE AIR

THE WITCH RUMMAGED THROUGH her cabinets, tossing aside vials of multi-colored liquids, sacks of pungent herbs, and a variety of tails, eyeballs, and claws. She pulled a small leather-bound book with decorative gold tooling from a shelf and flung it to the ground. "Useless," the witch mumbled. She stepped over the girl sobbing hysterically on the floor.

"Quiet! You are driving me mad!"

The girl let out a piercing scream, followed by even more frenzied sobs.

"You have only yourself to blame. Mother warned you not to take up with Hippolyta and her wenches. But you would not listen. And now look at you, Akantha. I do not know if I have the remedy to undue the damage caused by the gryphon."

"*Waah ah ah ah! Waaaaaaah!* I hate her!" Akantha shrieked.

"Oh, do not start with the daughter of Atlas! Again you did not heed Mother's warning," the witch said, kneeling next to Akantha. She grabbed Akantha's hair and pulled her head back. "Ugh! Your new look is going to take some getting used to."

"*WAAAAAAAAAAAAAAH!*"

"Now, now, that is enough. If Mother can transform a man into a pig, she can do something about your face."

The witch staggered to her feet and pushed open the wooden shutters covering a window. Sunlight filled the witch's house.

Akantha squealed and covered her face. The witch ignored her daughter and looked outside.

"There is a change in the air, daughter. Yes, I can sense it. Change has come once again to Olympia... and with it the opportunity to claim dominion. Bring yourself under control, daughter. Before this day is through, I will sit upon Lord Zeus's throne. And you will experience the dividends that patience can bring."

The End

APPENDIX

PEOPLE, PLACES & THINGS

ACROPOLIS – an ancient fortress in the city of Athens containing the ruins of several buildings, including the Parthenon and the temple of Athena Nike

ACHAEANS – a collective name for the Greeks who fought during the Trojan War

AEGLE – a nymph of the West and caretaker of the garden of the Hesperides

AKANTHA – the daughter of King Alphaios; taken in by the Amazons after his death; from the Greek word for "thorn" (o)

ALALA – a Greek battle cry; the daughter of Polemos

ALPHAIOS – a Greek king and the father of Akantha; former leader of a council to Zeus; took his life after being renounced by Zeus; from the Greek word for "changing" (o)

AMAZONS – a Greek tribe of mighty female warriors

AMPHISBAENA – a venomous, two-headed snake-like creature

APHRODITE – the Greek goddess of love and beauty

APOLLO – the Greek god of the sun

ATLAS

ATLAS – the Titan god of endurance and astronomy; father of the Pleiades and the nymphs of the West

AUTOLYCUS – a renowned Greek thief and trickster

CAPE SOUNION, GREECE – a promontory outside the city of Athens; location of the temple of Poseidon

CHARON – the ferryman of Hades who carried the dead to the Underworld

CHIMERA – a three-headed, fire-breathing creature made up of various animals

CIRCE – a Greek witch known for transforming her enemies into animals

COMUS – the Greek god of festivity and anarchy

CYCLOPS – a giant with a single eye in the middle of its forehead

DAEDALUS – a skilled craftsman and artist; father of Icarus; creator of the labyrinth on Crete

DORIAN TRIBE – a Greek tribe founded by the hero Doros; from the Greek "Dorios," meaning "child of the sea"

EOS – the Greek goddess of the dawn who opened the gates of heaven each morning

EURYSTHEUS – a Greek king who forced twelve labours upon Heracles

GAIA – the Greek mother goddess and personification of the Earth; mother of the Titans

GARDEN OF THE HESPERIDES – Hera's orchard in which were grown golden apples that granted immortality

GODS OF OLYMPUS – the twelve major gods of ancient Greece

GRYPHON – a creature with the body of a lion and head and wings of an eagle

HADES – the Greek god of the Underworld

HELIOS – the Greek personification of the sun

HEPHAESTUS – the Greek god of fire and metalworking

HERA – the Greek goddess of marriage and women; wife of Zeus; queen of the gods of Olympus

HERACLES – the demi-god son of Zeus and Alcmene

HIPPOLYTA – the queen of the Amazons

ICARUS – the son of Daedalus; known as "The boy who flew too close to the sun"

KRESTENA, GREECE – a town near the site of Olympia

LABOURS OF HERACLES – twelve tasks imposed upon Heracles as penance for killing his wife and children in a fit of madness

LADON – a massive serpentine dragon that guarded the garden of the Hesperides

LAMPUS – one of two horses that pulled the chariot of Eos across the arc of heaven

MAIA – the eldest of the Pleiades

NYMPHS OF THE WEST – female nature deities who tended the garden of the Hesperides; daughters of Atlas and Hesperius

OLYMPIA, GREECE – the site of the ancient Olympic games

OLYMPIA – a hidden world ruled by Zeus and the gods of Olympus populated by persons and creatures from Greek mythology (o)

PAN – the Greek god of nature and the wild

PANDORA'S BOX – a large jar that contained all the evils of the world

PENTHESILEA – an Amazon who died fighting in the Trojan War

PLEIADES – the seven daughters of Atlas and Pleione; transformed into stars by Zeus

POLEMOS - the Greek personification of war

POLYPHEMUS – a Cyclops and son of Poseidon

POSEIDON – the Greek god of the sea

SATYR – a half-man, half-goat creature

SCRYING POOL – a bowl of liquid used for divination or fortune-telling

SEA CLIFF, NEW YORK – a seaside village on the north shore of Long Island

TARTURUS – a deep abyss used as a dungeon and prison for the Titans

TITANOMACHY – a ten-year battle between the gods of Olympus and the Titans for control of the universe

TITANS – ancient Greek deities who preceded the gods of Olympus

TRITON – a Greek sea god; the son of Poseidon

TROJAN WAR – a great war waged against the city of Troy by the Achaeans

UNDERWORLD – the Greek otherworld where souls go after death; the realm of Hades

VARKIZA, GREECE – a seaside village outside the city of Athens

ZEUS – the Greek god of the sky and thunder; husband of Hera; father of Heracles; king of the gods of Olympus

(o) Denotes original concept

MAIA'S ADVENTURES IN OLYMPIA BEGAN IN...

MAIA *and* ICARUS

Maia Peterson was expecting the summer after seventh grade to be pretty uneventful. But when a fire destroys her home, she discovers a family secret that sends her halfway across the globe to Greece. Once there, Maia is whisked away to Olympia, a hidden world of mischievous mermaids, winged horses, and other creatures and characters from Greek mythology. And in this land out of time – where Zeus and his brethren still reign – Maia finds herself at the center of an age-old conflict between feuding gods.

With the aid of a legendary boy who flies too close to the sun, she battles against powerful forces determined to use her as a pawn. Along the way, she struggles to learn the truth about her heritage by solving the mystery of her father's disappearance. Will she be able to defy the fate others have planned for her? Will she dare to fly?

For more information, visit:
barrowcourtbooks.com

ACKNOWLEDGMENTS

MY SINCERE THANKS to everyone who supported the writing of *Maia and Hippolyta*, and especially to my husband, Eric; to my illustrator, Peter Prabowo; to my art director and designer, Michael Ebert; to my "pink kryptonite," Andie Ebert, and to my world-famous teacher friend, Erin Robilotta.

ABOUT *the* AUTHOR

JAMES A. PEREZ has worked in the field of education for over twenty years with children of all ages. He is a proud husband, father, and lifelong comic book fan who lives on Long Island with his family – including his niece, Maia.

In addition to *Maia and Icarus* and *Maia and Hippolyta*, he wrote *Grandpa's Walking Stick*, a picture book for his daughter, Ellie.